SHERLOCK BONES
AND THE MYSTERY OF THE VANISHING MAGICIAN

Published in Great Britain in 2023 by Buster Books,
an imprint of Michael O'Mara Books Limited,
9 Lion Yard, Tremadoc Road, London SW4 7NQ

W www.mombooks.com/buster

f Buster Books

y @BusterBooks

◎ buster_books

A CIP catalogue record for this book is available from the British Library.

ISBN: 978-1-78055-921-6

1 3 5 7 9 10 8 6 4 2

Papers used by Buster Books are natural, recyclable products
made of wood from well-managed, FSC®-certified forests and
other controlled sources. The manufacturing processes conform
to the environmental regulations of the country of origin.

This book was printed in April 2023 by
CPI Group (UK) Ltd, 108 Beddington Lane,
Croydon, CR0 4YY, United Kingdom.

SHERLOCK BONES
AND THE MYSTERY OF THE VANISHING MAGICIAN

Written by Tim Collins
Illustrated by John Bigwood

BUSTER BOOKS

With special thanks to Henry Collins – T. C.

To George and Oliver, may the greatest
adventures await – J. B.

Edited by Frances Evans
Designed by Derrian Bradder
Cover design by John Bigwood

Welcome

Sherlock Bones and Dr Jane Catson are world-famous for solving crimes. Each case is written down by Catson, so you can read all about their adventures.

Sherlock Bones

Sherlock Bones is the greatest detective the world has ever known. He never runs away from a puzzle, and always cracks his cases.

Dr Jane Catson

Dr Jane Catson is Sherlock Bones' crime-fighting partner. She's always ready to pounce into action when faced with a sneaky criminal.

Are you ready to help Bones and Catson solve their trickiest case yet? Throughout the story, you will find puzzles where you can put your own detective skills to the test. If you get stuck, you can find all the answers at the back of the book, starting on page 167. You can also just enjoy reading the adventure and come back to the puzzles later if you want to. Good luck!

Chapter One

The ginger cat pulled out a saw, and its sharp blade glinted in the light. He held it over the rabbit, who screamed and struggled.

"He's going to cut her in half!" I cried.

"Indeed," said Sherlock Bones. "And I know exactly how it's done. Let me explain, Catson ..."

"Please don't," I said. "You're sucking all the fun out of it."

We'd been watching The Great Otto's magic show for almost an hour, and Bones had ruined every single trick for me.

My friend's detective skills were great for cracking crimes, but I wished he'd give them a rest so I could watch the show. We'd been in Berlin all week, helping Archduke Rover find his golden fetching stick, and I just wanted to enjoy myself before we went back to London.

So far, Bones had worked out that the doves Otto had pulled out of thin air had actually been hidden under his top hat, and the string of handkerchiefs that had appeared in a puff of smoke had been stashed up his sleeve.

The magician sawed the side of the wooden box and his rabbit assistant wailed. The audience gasped and barked.

"Working out how these things are done IS the fun part, my dear Catson," said Bones. "In this case, you should have noticed that the rabbit's feet aren't moving."

Now that I stared at them, I could see the feet were models made from cardboard and felt.

"The rabbit's real body is hidden in a secret compartment below the box," said Bones. "It's all very simple."

The saw went all the way down, and the rabbit pretended to die. There were mews and whimpers from the crowd as the magician pulled the two halves of the box apart. A hare sobbed and blew into her handkerchief, while a hedgehog reached out and covered the eyes of her hoglets.

There was a moment of horrible silence, then the rabbit opened her eyes, and grinned. The crowd clapped and cheered, Otto pushed the two halves of the box back together, and the rabbit jumped out unharmed.

Otto brought out a single chair and stepped to the front of the stage. He had a top hat, a wide bow tie, and a smart black cloak with red lining.

"For the next part of the show, ladies and gentlemen, I shall need one of you to help me," he said, clasping his paws together. "That is to say, I am looking for a volunteer."

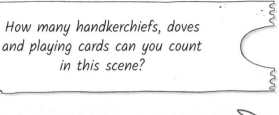

How many handkerchiefs, doves and playing cards can you count in this scene?

9

I shot my arm into the air. At least if I were on stage, Bones wouldn't be able to ruin things for me.

"Yes, madam," said the magician. "Please come up."

The crowd clapped as I made my way up the steps.

"And you are?" asked Otto.

"Dr Jane Catson," I said.

Otto pointed to the chair, and I sat down.

"I am about to demonstrate my greatest skill of all," said Otto. "Indeed, my most astounding. You shall now witness the power of hypnotism."

I sat down and looked out over the rows of dachshunds, pine martens and toads. A black cat on the front row had squeezed all her kittens on to one seat, and they were staring and mewing at me. I knew they'd all be disappointed when I didn't fall under the magician's spell, but what could I do? The trick simply wasn't going to work on me.

Otto whipped out a watch on a long gold chain, and swung it in front of my whiskers.

"Focus on the centre," he said. "That is to say, look at the middle. You are feeling very relaxed."

I tried to pick Bones out in the crowd to see if he was scoffing at us, but I couldn't take my gaze off the watch.

"Your eyelids are very heavy," said Otto. "You will close them in five … four … three … two … one …"

10

He clicked his fingers.

I felt my head droop forward and my eyes close. I tried to open them again, desperate not to fall for it.

With a great effort, I did it. I forced my eyelids apart.

I looked around the theatre. Everything had changed.

The whole place was empty. The Great Otto was gone, as well as Bones and the rest of the crowd. I stepped down from the stage and into the aisle.

"Hello?" I shouted. "Is anyone there?"

I lifted my paw to shield my eyes against the lights and saw a dark figure with long hair dashing out of the door. I felt like I had no choice but to follow.

I rushed forward, and shoved the door open, only to discover that I was in a completely different city. We'd been watching the magic show in Berlin. But now I was in Paris. I could see the lights of the Eiffel Tower rising above the dark street ahead of me.

The figure was running away. She turned back to look at me, and I saw she was a lemur with large black rings around her eyes, wearing an old-fashioned green dress.

She pelted down the street, moving faster than a cheetah who's desperate for a wee. I knew I'd have no chance of catching her, but I felt I had to try.

Which way should Catson go down the alleyways to catch up with the lemur? Avoid all the obstacles.

START

12

FINISH

13

I found myself turning into a side street on my right, and taking a winding path down dark alleyways to a crossroads with a green newspaper kiosk on the corner. The lemur was approaching from my left now. I'd taken a shortcut, and felt very pleased about this.

I pounced on the lemur, grabbing her by the waist. But she shrank beneath my grip until all that was left was her dress, and her long brown hair, which turned out to have been a wig.

I was staring at it in confusion when I heard the click of fingers, and the sound of hundreds of animals laughing.

"And you're back in the room," said Otto.

I opened my eyes. I was still in the theatre, where I'd been all along. I'd just pounced on a fluffy clockwork mouse, and the audience were finding it hilarious.

"Let's hear it for our volunteer, ladies and gentlemen," said Otto, clapping his paws. "That is to say, let's all thank her for being such a good sport."

I left the stage to loud applause. I was happy to have entertained the audience, even though I had no idea what I'd done.

Bones explained it all as we walked back to our hotel. "Otto said the toy mouse wanted to tell you something important, and you chased it all around the stage, with a very stern expression. I think even the magician was surprised at the speed of your pounce."

We passed under a huge stone gateway topped with a statue of a winged cat riding a chariot.

"I didn't feel like I was going after a mouse," I said. "I thought I was chasing a lemur with long brown hair. Do you think it means anything?"

"Nothing at all," said Bones. "Your brain just throws up random images when you're under hypnosis."

We arrived at our hotel, and the door doberman smiled and stepped aside. It was going to be a shame to leave this plush hotel and return to our messy kennel.

"So you believe hypnosis is real, then?" I asked. "I thought you'd say it was all nonsense."

"Of course it's real," said Bones. "It's a serious craft that takes years to learn. It might be performed by stage magicians, but it's no mere trick."

We were passing through the lobby when the German shepherd dog behind the counter held out a white envelope.

"Message for Mr Sherlock Bones!" she barked.

Bones grabbed the envelope and took out the letter inside.

"Anything important?" I asked.

"Not really," said Bones. "Our train tomorrow afternoon has been cancelled, so we'll have to take an overnight one to Paris and change there. It shouldn't add more than a few hours to our journey."

The image of the Eiffel Tower rising before me as I chased the lemur down the street shot back into my mind.

"Paris!" I cried. "That's the city I saw when I was hypnotized. This proves that my vision meant something after all!"

"It proves nothing," said Bones. "Except that your mind is racing, and you need to sleep."

Whatever Bones thought, I was convinced my brain was somehow trying to warn me. Something strange was going to happen to us in Paris. I was sure of it.

Chapter Two

We arrived at the train station the next evening. A black locomotive with neat red carriages chugged into the platform, sending up thick puffs of smoke.

The door of the front carriage came to a stop in front of two sloths who were carrying heavy suitcases. A large bear and moose were behind them, and groups of elephants, shrews and gibbons crushed forward to get on board.

"It looks as though lots of other animals have had their trains cancelled," I said. "I hope we don't have to stand up all night."

The lynx guard opened the door and the sloths slowly climbed in. The bear and moose followed, and all the other animals crammed in afterwards.

We dashed to the door at the back, and leapt on.

Each carriage had three compartments with six seats, and a narrow corridor running down the left side.

The back carriage was taken by a wombat, a weasel, a hairless cat and a polecat, the next by a family of elephants, and the next by a family of pygmy shrews.

We spotted one carriage with a few free seats, so we dashed in before anyone else could grab them. There was a cow sitting on the left with a huge bag of grass on her lap. Next to her was a skunk, and opposite them was a hyena reading a book.

I took the window seat next to the skunk. Bones took the one opposite me, and got out his *Bumper Book of Pawprints*.

A whistle blew, and the train lurched forward.

It soon became clear why no one else had wanted the seats. The skunk next to me was giving off a horrible eggy waft. The hyena was reading a joke book and screeching out an annoying laugh after each gag. And the cow was shovelling grass into her mouth and chewing noisily.

Can you spot seven differences between the pictures of Bones and Catson's compartment?

I wondered how I'd ever sleep with all this commotion going on. But then I remembered Bones' book.

I reached over and tapped him.

"Could you read some of that out to me?" I asked.

"Certainly," said Bones. He cleared his throat. "The upper pads of the American bulldog are slightly thinner than those of the French bulldog. The breed is also a little heavier, meaning deeper impressions are made in sand, snow and mud …"

As Bones droned on, I felt my head drooping forward. The laughter of the hyena and the chewing of the cow faded, and the reek of the skunk seemed to float away.

When I opened my eyes, it was completely dark. For a moment, I struggled to remember where I was, or why I was hurtling rapidly backwards.

I looked out of the window, and saw the dark outlines of distant hills. There were no streaks of dawn in the sky yet. I'd have to try and get back to sleep, but it wasn't going to be easy in the uncomfortable train seat.

I massaged the back of my head and looked at the others.

The hyena, the skunk and the cow were all fast asleep,

and Bones had nodded off with his book open. Perhaps he'd bored himself to sleep, too.

I was about to close my eyes again when I noticed there was another figure in the compartment with us.

A ginger cat was sitting by the door. I knew I'd seen him before, but couldn't quite work out who he was in my confused state. It was only when I saw his wide bow tie that I realized it was The Great Otto.

He waved at me, and I noticed that his paw was trembling.

"Nice to see you again," he whispered.

He glanced out at the corridor with his ears pinned back.

"What are you doing here?" I asked. "I thought you performed your show every night."

"I shan't be making the next one," he said. "I've run into a spot of trouble. Indeed, there has been rather an emergency."

I tried to ask him about it, but found myself yawning instead.

He took his hat off and pulled out a fluffy fake dove.

"Use this as a pillow, if you like," he said. "It might help you get back to sleep."

"Thanks," I said, taking the dove and propping it against the window. It was much better than slumping forward. "Are you sure you don't want it yourself?"

"Positive," he whispered. "That is to say, I don't think I'll be getting much sleep tonight anyway."

I wanted to ask him what was worrying him so much, but all that came out were murmurs. I was drifting off again.

I woke to bright sunshine and had to loosen my scarf to cool down. We were speeding past dense pine forests, broken up by flat fields and wonky farmhouses. We zoomed into a tunnel, and were plunged into darkness for a few seconds.

My mouth felt like the inside of a litter tray, and I realized I must have been in a deep sleep.

The cow was chewing her morning grass, and the skunk was nibbling on spider cheese, rotten herring and raw garlic.

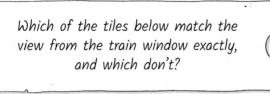

Which of the tiles below match the view from the train window exactly, and which don't?

A. B. C. D.

E. F. G. H.

Opposite me, the hyena was trying out some of her jokes on Bones.

"What type of dog is best at telling the time?" she asked.

"That's an interesting question," said Bones, stroking his chin. "I find that border collies are very punctual. Is that the answer?"

"A watch-dog," said the hyena. She threw her head back and howled with laughter, but Bones failed to crack a smile.

"I see," he said. "Interesting."

My friend might be a brilliant detective, but he's not great with jokes. I once took him to see the tiger comedian Stripy Rogers, and he spent all night jotting things in his notebook without so much as a giggle.

"Try this one," said the hyena. "Why did the magician love trapdoors?"

Everything that had happened in the night came flooding back to me.

"I've just remembered," I said. "The Great Otto was in this carriage last night."

I pointed to the empty seat next to the corridor.

"He was right there."

"Are you sure?" asked Bones. "I was awake by six and I saw no sign of him."

"Yes," I said. "I'm positive."

Bones stood up and clapped his paws together.

"Excuse me, fellow passengers," he said. "Did anyone else see a ginger cat with a top hat and a wide bow tie in this carriage last night?"

"No," said the hyena.

"Nah," said the skunk, opening a jar of pickled onions.

"Absolutely not," said the cow, shoving an extra handful of grass into her mouth.

Bones sat down again.

"So, there we have it," he said. "One animal in this compartment saw him, and four did not. The most likely explanation is that you dreamt the magician was here. It's no wonder he was on your mind after your recent experience."

I wondered if Bones was right. Being hypnotized had been very odd, and I'd been thinking about it a lot.

Yet it had felt so real. If it had been a dream, something weird would have happened, like The Great Otto would have turned into my Aunt Ruby, or I'd suddenly have realized I was back in school and about to sit my mice-catching exam. But we'd just had an ordinary conversation, and I could remember the whole thing.

I decided to stop worrying and get some more rest. I placed my fluffy dove against the window and was about to close my eyes when I gasped and bolted upright again.

"Wait a minute," I said, holding up the dove to show Bones. "The Great Otto gave me this. This proves he was really here."

Bones examined the dove with his magnifying glass.

"Extraordinary," he said.

28

"It was just a stage he was going through," said the hyena.

I exchanged a puzzled glance with Bones.

"That's why the magician loved trapdoors," said the hyena. "Get it?"

She threw her head back and laughed.

Chapter Three

"It seems our magician must have been here, after all," said Bones. "No doubt he got restless in the night and changed carriages. Let's go and find him."

We started at the back of the train and worked our way forward. Each carriage was packed with animals who were sleeping, reading, chatting, gazing out of the window or munching snacks. But there was no sign of Otto.

"Well, well," said Bones. "It looks as though we might have an interesting situation on our paws."

We ended up in the dining car at the front of the train. The lynx guard was rushing down the aisle and placing menus between the salt and ground-insect cellars on the tables. She was wearing a yellow apron over her blue uniform.

"Sorry, you'll have to wait for breakfast until nine," she said. "I'm so behind with everything."

"We don't need to eat," said Bones. "We just need to ask you two questions."

I made the mistake of glancing at the menu and noticed that smoked salmon was on it. My stomach rumbled.

Can you put the salt and ground-insect cellars into matching pairs?

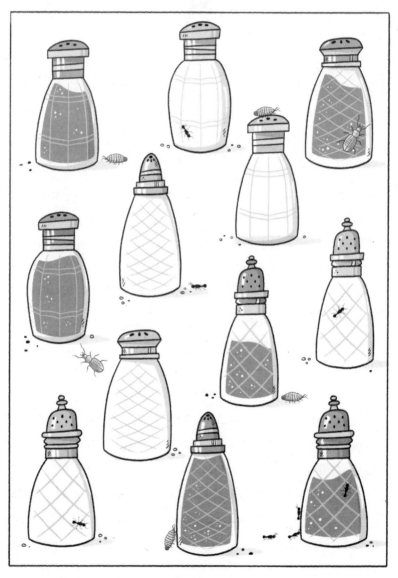

"Okay, but make it quick," said the guard. "I've been rushed off my feet today. The chef is off sick, so I've got to make the breakfast as well as check the tickets. And on such a crowded journey, too."

"Firstly, have you seen a ginger cat on this train?" asked Bones. "Wearing a black cape, a top hat and a wide bow tie."

The guard paused in the middle of propping up a menu.

"No," she said. "Haven't seen anyone like that."

"And has this train stopped at all since we left Berlin?" asked Bones.

"Definitely not," said the guard. "We're making good time. At least that's something."

The guard walked back towards the small kitchen area at the end of the carriage, but Bones rushed ahead and blocked her way.

"I need you to stop the train right now," he said. "And call the local police."

The guard burst out laughing.

"You've got to be joking," she said. "I'm already struggling to cope with all the passengers. The last thing I need is to delay them."

"A cat has gone missing from this train," said Bones. "I hardly think he would have jumped off on purpose. We need to work out what's happened."

The guard pushed past Bones and grabbed a box of spoons.

"When did you last see him?" she asked.

"As a matter of fact, I didn't," said Bones. "But Dr Catson here saw him in the middle of the night, and I trust everything she says."

The guard sighed and rolled her eyes.

"It was probably just a dream," she said. "I can't stop the train and tell the police to find someone who might never have been here at all. Why don't you go and talk to the other passengers? If they remember the cat too, I'll see what I can do."

We walked back out into the corridor. Bones examined the windows and doors with his magnifying glass as we made our way down it.

"Someone else is bound to have seen Otto," I said. "There's no way I can have been the only one."

"I certainly hope so," said Bones. "But we need to be very careful. I'd much rather we'd have stopped the train and got the police involved before talking to everyone. What if

someone deliberately pushed him out? They won't like us asking questions."

I drew my claws and tensed my muscles. If any villains tried to attack, I'd be ready.

The first compartment was taken up by three beavers and two gibbons. None of them had seen Otto.

The next housed a goat, two red pandas, a leopard and a squirrel, and they couldn't help us either.

The next was the one the sloths had chosen, as well as the bear and moose. The sloths were asleep, and I didn't think it was worth waking them. Knowing sloths, they'd have been dozing ever since we left Berlin anyway.

The moose's antlers were so big that they went up through the metal luggage rack above him and cradled his suitcase. When we asked if he'd seen Otto, he shook his head so vigorously that it looked like the suitcase was about to fall off.

The bear was reading a Paris guidebook. She looked up from it and grunted, "No".

Can you work out which attraction the bear is looking at? The letters written at the bottom of the page can be rearranged to spell out a clue.

5 MUST-SEE ATTRACTIONS

3. VENUS DE FIDO

1. EIFFEL TOWER

4. ARC DE TRIOMPHE

2. SACRÉ-COEUR

5. NOTRE-DAME

ATUETS

We came to the toilet compartment next, and Bones insisted we look inside. There were twelve litter trays of different sizes, and most had been used already. I held my nose as we entered.

Bones took out his magnifying glass and crouched down.

"I doubt The Great Otto would want to hide in any of those," I said. "Unless he accidentally sawed his own brain in half."

"That doesn't mean there won't be important clues," said Bones.

He examined the trays at the back.

"These things that look like rotten coconuts are elephant dung," he said. "These small brown pellets are shrew droppings. And these cubic poos are from a wombat. They're the only animals who poo in that shape, you know."

"Great," I said. "Can we go now?"

We moved on, and I could finally breathe again.

We passed our compartment, where the cow and skunk were still eating, and the hyena was still screeching, and moved on to the pygmy shrews and elephants. None of them had seen anything.

Finally, we approached the last compartment. Through the glass, I could see a weasel sitting by the window who was holding a newspaper close to his face, and a hairless cat sitting next to him. On the opposite seats were a polecat and a wombat.

"Let's hope this lot can help," said Bones. "Because if they can't, we're completely stuck."

Bones opened the door and clapped his paws together.

"I wonder if you can help us?" he asked. "We're looking for a ginger cat wearing a top hat and a wide bow tie."

The polecat rubbed her eyes, smoothing out circles in her fur.

"No," she said. "Sorry."

The weasel lowered his newspaper and said "No".

The wombat shrugged his shoulders.

"Think carefully," said Bones. "He was in our carriage last night, so he must have walked right past here. Are you sure none of you saw anything?"

The polecat took a pair of round glasses out of her jacket pocket.

"I didn't have these on," she said. "So I wouldn't have seen him anyway."

The wombat pointed to his pillow, which was next to him on the seat.

"I've been asleep since we set off," he said. "I only woke up ten minutes ago, so I can't help."

"We were awake all night and didn't see him," said the hairless cat, pulling some stray ginger hairs from her left sleeve. She pointed to the weasel on her right. "And my husband Gunter here has terrific eyesight, so he misses nothing."

The weasel nodded in agreement.

"Thank you all," said Bones.

He closed the door and we continued down to the very end of the train. There was nothing left but the door we'd boarded from, and an identical one opposite. Unless The Great Otto was clinging to the roof, our search had come to nothing.

"Looks like we've drawn a blank," I said.

"A blank?" asked Bones. "Don't tell me you didn't pick up on any of those clues?"

I thought back over our walk down the train. I hadn't noticed a single one.

Chapter Four

Bones brought his paws together and rested his nose on them. Steep hills covered in dark green trees were flying past outside.

"My dear Catson," he said. "If you'd been paying any attention at all, you'd have noticed that every single animal in that last carriage was lying."

He pointed to the fur around his eyes.

"Firstly, the polecat said she couldn't have seen anything because she hadn't been wearing her glasses. Yet, when I first asked about Otto, she smoothed down the fur around her eyes. She was removing the marks her glasses had made and getting ready to lie to us."

I thought back to when I'd first seen her. Bones was right.

"But why did she want to mislead us?" I asked.

"Because she DID see something," said Bones. "She just didn't want to tell us about it. Next, the wombat told us he hadn't left the compartment all night. But remember those cubic poos we saw in the litter tray? He must have done them, as there are no other wombats on board."

I was glad our visit to the toilet compartment hadn't been wasted after all. At least the smell I'd endured hadn't been for nothing.

"The hairless cat claimed her husband had great eyesight, yet he was holding his newspaper close to his face, just as someone with poor vision would. And while she was talking to us, she pulled a few hairs from her left sleeve. Yet the seat on her left was empty, and the hairs can hardly have come from her."

It was bad enough that I hadn't spotted the other clues, but this one was unforgivable. Of course a hairless cat couldn't have moulted on her own clothes! Even the silliest kitten could have worked that out.

"The Great Otto was in that compartment," said Bones. "You mark my words. They all saw him, and none of them want to admit it. Let's find out why."

We strode back into the compartment and I stood in front of the door so none of the animals could make a run for it.

"I'm terribly sorry," said Bones. "I forgot to introduce myself earlier. I'm the detective Sherlock Bones and I know liars when I see them. I'm looking at a bunch of them right now."

The hairless cat hissed and arched her back.

"Look what you've done to my poor wife!" yelled the weasel. "This is playing havoc with her nerves. You have no right to make crazy accusations about us!"

He looked to the polecat and wombat for support, but they just sighed and looked down at their feet.

"It was my square poos, wasn't it?" said the wombat. "I wish I could do round ones like other animals."

"Never mind how I worked it out," said Bones. "Why were you lying? Are you involved in a catnapping conspiracy?"

The polecat gasped and leapt up from her seat.

"Of course not," she said. "We'd never do anything like that. The truth is that we did see your ginger cat last night, but we didn't want to say anything in the case the guard came to see us, because ... well ... we don't have tickets."

The hairless cat flushed red and pulled out a fan to cool herself down.

"And we don't have enough money to pay for tickets if the guard catches us," said the wombat. "We're worried she'll kick us off the train, and we really need to get to Paris."

"We're artists, you see," said the hairless cat. "But no one in Berlin understood our work, so we didn't sell any paintings. I'm sure we'll have much more success in Paris."

The weasel got up and pulled a suitcase down from the metal rails. He flipped it open to reveal a painting of a hillside that looked like a green pile  of cat vomit, a seaside landscape with strange grey blobs that were probably meant to be seagulls, a fruit bowl where the oranges were for some reason bigger than the bananas, and a portrait of the hairless cat that made her look like an elderly giraffe.

"No one in Berlin wanted to buy any of these," he said. "Can you believe it?"

I found it very easy to believe, as a matter of fact. These were some of the worst paintings I'd even seen.

"We could do a portrait of you two," said the wombat. "If you give us enough money to buy our tickets."

"Certainly not," said Bones. "In fact, I'm considering telling the guard about you right now. Tell us exactly what happened last night, and I want the truth this time."

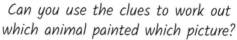

Can you use the clues to work out which animal painted which picture?

- The wombat did not paint the seaside picture.

- The polecat's painting has a thick frame.

- The weasel's painting is the only one without animals in it.

- The hairless cat's painting is set indoors.

A.

B.

C.

D.

The wombat pointed to the empty seat by the door.

"A ginger cat just like the one you were describing rushed on to the train as it was leaving, and sat down there," he said.

"He kept looking out into the corridor, like he was scared," said the polecat.

Bones crouched down and examined the empty seat with his magnifying glass.

"He seemed distracted," said the hairless cat. "He wasn't at all interested in seeing our art."

This made him sensible rather than distracted as far as I was concerned, but I let them go on.

"He was there when we went to sleep," said the weasel. "And when we woke up, he was gone."

"Interesting," said Bones. "Sounds like he was frightened of someone. I wonder who?"

Bones pulled the door aside.

"We'll be back shortly," he said.

I followed Bones out into the corridor. The bear we'd seen earlier was standing in it and we had to squeeze past her.

"Great work," I said, as we rushed to the dining compartment. "The guard will have to stop the train now we've got witnesses."

We found the lynx guard in the kitchen area at the back of the dining cart, cutting a round loaf of bread.

The lynx wants to slice this loaf into eight equal pieces using just three cuts. How can she do it?

"We've found four other animals who saw the cat," I said. "Come with us."

The guard sighed.

"Does it have to be right now?" she asked. "I was just about to ring the bell for breakfast."

"A cat has gone missing from your train," said Bones. "Something terrible might have happened, and it's high time you took it seriously."

"Fine," said the guard. She took her apron off and tossed it on to a chair.

We led her down to the last compartment, and she grumbled under her breath all the way.

We slid the door aside and strode in.

The artists were still sitting in their seats, but they didn't turn to look at us.

"Right," said Bones. "Tell the guard what you just told us."

The weasel exchanged a confused glance with the hairless cat.

"I'm sorry," he said. "I don't understand what you mean."

"Tell the guard about the ginger cat," I said. "The one who went missing last night."

The hairless cat shrugged.

"We haven't seen any ginger cats," she said. "Perhaps you're confusing us with some other animals."

The wombat and the polecat looked out of the window and said nothing.

I was so angry I could hardly speak.

"You just told us you saw the cat!" I hissed. "Why have you started lying again?"

The lynx threw up her paws.

"I haven't got time for this," she said. "If you need me, I'll be in the dining carriage. But don't bother me until you've found some genuine witnesses."

She turned to go, but the weasel stood up and stuck his hand in his pocket.

"Actually, there is one thing you could help us with," he said. "I'm afraid we all boarded this train without tickets because we were in a rush. Could we buy them now?"

The weasel pulled out a large wad of banknotes and started to count them.

"Fine," said the guard. "But let's make this quick. You really should have bought them at the station."

She took a book of tickets and a pen out of her pocket and began scribbling.

· COMPAGNIE INTERNATIONALE ·

Nº 0703 · PAWRIENT EXPRESS · Nº 0703

Chapter Five

We made our way back to the dining cart when the lynx rang the bell for breakfast. I finally got to eat some of the smoked salmon, and hoped it would be easier to think on a full stomach.

The artists sauntered in soon after us and sat two tables away. They ordered everything on the menu and threw a wad of notes at the guard.

"So much for them being poor," I said. "I wonder why they lied about it?"

"I don't think they did," said Bones. "I'm pretty sure they were telling the truth when they said they had no money. They've only just got their paws on some cash. They're wasting it, as many animals do when they suddenly find themselves richer."

The wombat glugged down a glass of orange juice and asked the guard for another one.

Can you work out the price of the following items of food using the total cost next to each animal's plate? The price of each item is different. All the prices are whole numbers and no item is worth more than €8.

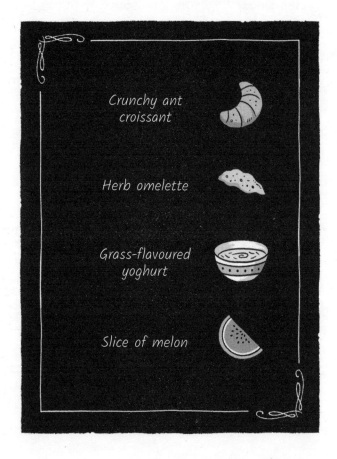

Crunchy ant croissant

Herb omelette

Grass-flavoured yoghurt

Slice of melon

55

"How can you get rich on a speeding train?" I asked. "You don't think they stole it, do you?"

"No," said Bones. "Which makes it all the more puzzling. They seemed genuinely ashamed when they admitted they didn't have tickets. I don't think they'd look so brash if they'd just picked someone's pockets."

Bones looked around at all the other tables.

"Someone gave them the money," he said. "But who? And how is it related to Otto's disappearance?"

I looked across the carriage. The cow was drinking her daisy smoothie, the pygmy shrew family were eating tiny spider omelettes, and the elephants were enjoying their leaves on toast. Were any of them secret criminals?

"Let's get back to our compartment," said Bones, standing up. "I need my chewing bones."

My friend carries his collection of rubber bones everywhere in case he has a tricky case to chew over. Some days it takes him hours of gnawing to get anywhere. I hoped this wouldn't be one of them. I had a feeling Otto needed our help.

I looked in at all the carriages as we passed. Many of the animals had stayed inside them instead of going to breakfast.

The gibbons had the first carriage to themselves, and were taking the chance to swing from the luggage racks.

56

The leopard and goat were staring out of the window of the next carriage, playing 'I-Spy'.

In the third carriage, the sloths were still fast asleep, the bear was still reading and the moose was still sitting opposite her, with his suitcase shuffling around above his antlers.

Back in our carriage, the hyena and skunk had gone to sleep again, which was a relief. The silence would make it easier for Bones to concentrate.

We tiptoed past and took our seats. Bones grabbed a huge rubber bone from his case and chewed on it.

I slouched back and tried to think my way through the problem, but I couldn't focus. I was still too annoyed with myself for failing to pick up on all those clues earlier. I'd been helping Bones crack cases for years now and should have noticed them.

If only I could spot another clue that Bones had missed, it would make up for it. But I'd seen nothing.

An image came into my mind, and I sat bolt upright. Maybe I had seen something after all. A shiver ran up my tail as I thought back to what I'd seen in the third carriage. The sloths had been asleep, just like before. The bear had been reading, just like before. The moose had been sitting opposite him, just like before. The case had been moving above him, just like before.

But this time, the moose hadn't been shuffling his antlers. The case had been moving all on its own.

I grabbed Bones' paw, and he almost spat out his rubber bone in shock.

"It's the moose!" I said. "He's the one we need to question. There's something weird going on with his suitcase!"

Bones threw his chewing bone down to the seat.

"Good heavens!" he said. "You're right!"

We raced back along the train.

The moose spotted us coming and started fidgeting around in his seat again, rocking the case with his antlers.

We stepped into the carriage and closed the door behind us.

"We're still searching for the ginger cat," said Bones. "Are you sure you haven't seen him?"

The moose shook his head, rattling his case further.

"Nothing has changed since we last spoke," he said. "I'll let you know if it does."

I moved closer to the case. There was a strange, muffled noise coming from inside.

The bear stood up. She was so tall she had to bend her head to avoid hitting the roof.

"We've helped all we can," she said. "Now why don't you go back to your own carriage and stop bothering us?"

I felt my fur prickle. So, the bear and moose were working together. But what exactly were they up to? I needed to get the suitcase open. I crouched down, wiggled my bottom from side to side, and pounced up to the luggage rack. It was made from three metal slats joined at the ends and in the middle, and was tough to balance on.

I scrabbled along as the moose tried to swat at me. His huge hoof slapped down right next to my tail, but I managed to reach the case, and flick open the latches.

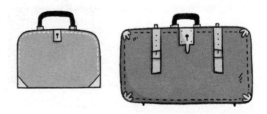

I couldn't stop myself from gasping. The Great Otto was trapped inside, with his paws tied and a gag over his mouth. He looked at me with wide eyes as I reached for the rope binding his wrists together.

There was a roar behind me and I felt a strong grip on my waist. The bear yanked me down from the shelf and dangled me in the middle of the carriage. She grabbed Bones in her other paw and held him up, too.

We kicked and struggled against the brute's grip, but she was too strong.

"Help!" I cried. "We're being attacked!"

There was no one in the corridor, and the clattering of the train was drowning out my cries.

The moose slammed the suitcase shut and fastened the latches.

I took a deep breath and let out the loudest scream I could. I looked around and saw one of the sloths had opened his eyes.

"Please help us!" I cried. "Attack these villains!"

"Give me a minute," said the sloth.

He dragged himself up with his long arms until he was standing on the seat. He bunched his paws into fists and fixed his eyes on the bear.

"Stop that," he said, letting out a yawn. "Or you'll have me to …"

The sloth collapsed down on the seat, fast asleep.

"Thanks," I said. "Great rescuing."

Bones struck his paw into the bear's underarm and tickled her, but she didn't react. I drew my claws and dug them into her arm, but she didn't loosen her grip at all. We were clearly dealing with a true, hardened criminal.

"I can see these two are going to be trouble," she said. "Clear some space."

The moose reached up to the luggage rack opposite him and took down two suitcases. He unzipped them, and I saw the terrible paintings the artists had shown us earlier. He grabbed the ones of the hills, the seaside and the fruit bowl, and threw them out of the window. He was about to do the same with the cat portrait, but the bear shook her head.

Which silhouette matches
the moose exactly?

A.

B.

C.

D.

E.

F.

"Keep that," she said. "I've got something in mind for it."

With the paintings gone, there was plenty of room for us inside the cases.

I could now see exactly what had happened, and I felt silly for not working it out sooner. While the artists had confessed their dishonesty to us, the bear had been listening from the corridor.

When we'd gone to fetch the guard, she must have gone into their compartment and offered to buy their terrible paintings for full price if they promised to pretend they'd never seen Otto when the guard came back.

I hoped the artists had seen their rotten paintings flying out of the window. They deserved it.

I tried to wriggle free as the bear pushed us into the open cases.

Chapter Six

I writhed against the bear's grip as she shoved us down.
The sharp points of her claws dug deep into my sides as
I struggled.

I put both my paws around her little finger, and yanked
it back. It worked. The bear yelped, and loosened her grip
just enough for me to escape.

I managed to roll off the case and on to the seat next
to it. The bear let go of Bones and lunged for me with
both paws.

Everything went dark. It took me a few moments to
realize we'd entered a tunnel.

"Bones!" I hissed. "Make for the roof. They won't be able
to follow us out of the window. I'll get Otto."

I drew myself back on the seat and wiggled my haunches.
Then I pounced up to the luggage rack opposite. I scrabbled
along and opened the case containing Otto, reached in and
untied his paws and feet. I was just about to take off his gag
when daylight flooded back in. We were out of the tunnel.

The bear spun around and grabbed at me. She slammed

her huge paw down, but I managed to dodge aside, dragging Otto with me.

I looked over to the window and saw Bones clambering out. He landed on the roof above us with a thud.

"Follow him!" I cried, giving Otto a firm shove.

The moose stepped in front of the window. I think he was trying to block it, but he actually made things easier. Otto clambered over his antlers as if he were climbing a tree, and scrabbled up to the roof, too.

Now there was just me left. The bear lunged for me, but the sloth stretched his foot out in his sleep, and tripped her over. She crashed down, accidentally pulling the moose over, too. It looked as though the sloth had come to my rescue, after all.

I took my chance, pouncing out of the window, grabbing the metal frame, and spinning myself upwards.

I landed on the top of the carriage, and tried to get my balance as the train rattled around.

There were wide metal ridges lining the roof. I squatted down, gripped one and took a moment to get my breath back.

Follow the pawprints in the order given to help Bones, Catson and Otto climb along the roof. You can go up, down and across but not diagonally.

ORDER TO FOLLOW:

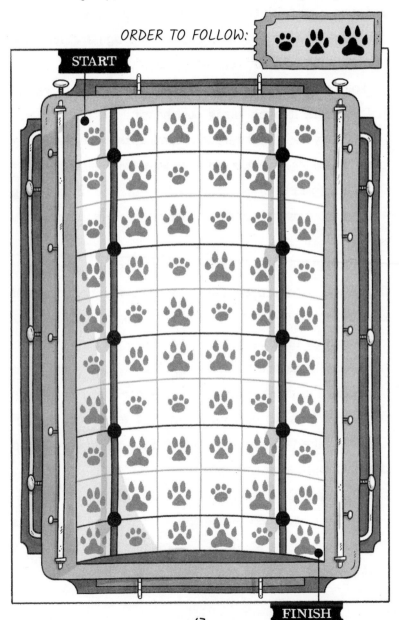

Bones was grasping the one ahead with one paw, while reaching over to untie Otto's gag with the other.

"Thank you both so much," said the magician. "I'd shake your paws if I could."

An overhanging tree scraped across the train, and we had to cling tight to avoid being pushed off.

"Let's try to get forward and climb down into the dining cart," I said. "The guard will have to believe us now."

We managed to drag ourselves along the roof by grabbing the ridges. Steep hillsides and dark forests whipped past on either side of us.

I reached the end of the carriage and got to my feet. There was a small gap between the carriage and the next one. I was sure we could make it, as long as no sudden gusts of wind blew us off.

I jumped over and looked back to see if Bones and Otto would do the same. What I saw made my blood freeze.

The bear was climbing on to the roof at the very back of the train. She'd opened the door and was pulling herself up with her thick arms.

"Come on!" I cried. "Hurry!"

The bear stomped along the roof. To the passengers inside, it must have sounded like boulders were falling on it. Surely someone would hear the noise and alert the guard?

Bones and Otto yelped and got to their feet. They clung on to their hats as they jumped over the gap, and raced along the carriages. There was no time to crawl now. We'd have to take our chances and try to get to the dining cart before the bear caught us.

Otto yelped and pointed ahead.

"This could be a problem," he said. "Indeed, it does not look good."

I gasped. The mouth of a tunnel was approaching.

"Get down!" I cried.

I pushed myself flat against the roof and Bones and Otto did the same. Terrifying though it was to hurtle towards an arch of solid brick, I could see how it might help us. We could fit in the narrow gap between the train roof and the underside of the tunnel. The bear could not.

We flew into the tunnel and were plunged into darkness. Thick plumes of smoke swept over us, stinging my eyes and filling my mouth with a horrible, sooty taste.

In seconds, we were back in bright daylight. I looked behind and saw the bear was gone.

Using these clues, can you work out which tunnel the train went through?

- *The tunnel is made from brick.*

- *The entrance is a rounded arch.*

- *More than one railway track runs through it.*

A.

B.

C.

D.

E.

F.

I let out a long sigh. One of our problems was out of the way. Now we just had the moose to deal with.

"Err ... I'm afraid that might not have been the success we hoped for," said Otto.

He was pointing to the back of the train. The thick paws of the bear were rising over it again. She must have dashed back and clung to the end of the carriage before we hit the tunnel.

She pulled herself back up and bounded towards us.

"What now?" asked Bones.

I looked ahead, desperately hoping another tunnel was on the way. But we were passing through flat farmland that was broken up only by a line of trees.

I got to my feet and bunched my paws into fists.

"We fight," I said.

Otto stood up beside me and drew his wand from his pocket. Bones took to his feet and drew his magnifying glass.

The bear pulled herself up to her full height, threw her paws back and stuck out her thick yellow claws.

I gulped. Maybe this wasn't such a good idea after all. The bear was about to swat us off the train like flies.

Chapter Seven

As the bear charged towards us, I looked over my shoulder and saw that we were about to pass an overhanging tree.

"Change of plan," I said. "Let's jump into that tree instead."

I grabbed a low branch. Otto and Bones grasped two other ones. Our weight dragged the tree down, and we had to scrabble up it as it brushed the train.

I heard the bear growling and snatching at the branches, and for a moment I thought she was going to jump into the tree and join us. But a second later, the train had gone, leaving just a plume of smoke.

I peered through the leaves and saw her roaring on the end of the last carriage as it sped away.

We'd rescued Otto from the bear, though I had no idea where we were or what we were going to do next.

I climbed down the trunk and brushed some twigs from my coat and scarf. We were at the edge of a wide green field that led to a single-track road.

Otto came down after me.

"Feeling alright?" I asked.

"Absolutely," he said. "That is to say, I'm unharmed. And I am very grateful to you for rescuing me. But it would have been much better if we were still on that train. For there is now no one to stop that bear and moose from carrying out one of the most fiendish crimes in history."

I slumped down with my head in my paws. I was hoping I might get some rest after the ordeal on the roof, but it seemed our problems were just beginning.

Bones leapt down next to me and grinned.

"Excellent," he said. "That's just how we like it."

He grabbed Otto's paw and shook it.

"I'm Sherlock Bones," he said. "You've already met Dr Jane Catson, of course. And there's nothing we love more than thwarting crimes. Tell us more."

Otto smoothed out his jacket and adjusted his hat.

"Very well," he said, pacing up and down and waving his paws as if he were on stage. "Let me set the scene for you. I was performing in the theatre last night, and reached the very part of my show that you volunteered for the previous night, Dr Catson. That is to say, it was time to astound the gathered animals with my powers of hypnosis."

He lifted his right paw, and I saw he now had the pocket watch in it, though I hadn't seen him take it out.

75

"But there was a difference last night," he said. "Sadly, no one was brave enough to step up, so I was forced to choose someone. My eyes were drawn to a bear and moose. That is to say, the very bear and moose we have just been dealing with. I invited the bear onstage, and she reluctantly came up."

The magician mimed pushing a chair out.

"She grumbled that the trick would not work on her," he said. "The ones who say that are the ones it works most easily on, I find."

I felt my cheeks heating up. This is exactly what I'd told myself before I'd been hypnotized.

"She was soon under my spell and I started by asking about her job," said Otto. "She said she was a robber, and

the crowd laughed, assuming it was a joke. But I knew she couldn't lie under hypnosis, and that I'd stumbled across something very dangerous."

Bones was jigging up and down with excitement.

"What kind of robbers are they?" he asked. "What is this great crime they're planning?"

Otto held his paw up.

"I am just about to reveal that very thing," he said. "I asked the bear what was she was going to do next, and she revealed she'd just got a letter from 'the boss', and she was on her way to Paris ... to steal the *Mona Lemur*!"

I gasped. The *Mona Lemur* was the most famous, and most valuable, painting in the world. Surely no criminals would be bold enough to swipe it?

Can you find the co-ordinates for these close-ups of the Mona Lemur?

A. B. C. D. E.

"I carried on with my act, making her chase a toy mouse around the stage to great amusement," said Otto. "I then snapped her out of it and sent her back to her seat. The crowd roared and clapped at what they thought was a brilliant prank. But I knew I'd uncovered a hideous crime. When the show finished, I followed them out of the theatre. I knew I had to try and stop them, though I had no idea how."

Otto leapt around, miming tiptoeing and looking from side to side.

"Hiding in the shadows, and sneaking forward without a sound, I followed them to the station. I bought a ticket to Paris and made it on to the train just as it was setting off. It was a big sacrifice for me, as I knew I would have to miss my show tonight and disappoint my loyal fans. I can only hope that my understudy, The Quite-Good Karl, does a decent job."

Otto drew his paws together and fixed his eyes on us.

"I hung back in the last compartment, hoping to go unseen," he said. "But a weasel insisted on sketching my portrait, and I was worried the villains might see it and recognize me, so I moved along the train, to where I saw you."

Otto needn't have worried. The portrait would have looked nothing like him, so it wouldn't have mattered who'd have seen it.

"In the early hours of the morning, when I was sure everyone would be asleep, I set off for the front of the train," he said. "I intended to find the guard, and tell her to bring us to a stop and call the police. I thought I'd spotted the guard when I saw a dark figure at the end of the corridor. I strode towards it, only to find the bear charging out of the shadows towards me."

Otto grabbed the back of his neck and mimed pulling himself up.

"She lifted me by the neck, like a mother with a naughty kitten," he said. "I tried to fight, but she was too strong. Soon, the moose was awake, and clearing space inside his suitcase by throwing his pyjamas and antler-warmers out of the window. I was shoved inside, and would still be there now if it weren't for you brave crime-fighters."

Otto bowed, and Bones clapped his paws together.

"Well, well," he said. "This is a most unusual case. I'm often consulted when something valuable has been stolen, but rarely am I consulted when something is about to be stolen. And the *Mona Lemur*, of all things."

I looked around. There was no one in the field or on the tiny road. We were stuck in the middle of nowhere, while the criminals were closing in on Paris. How on earth were we going to stop them?

Chapter Eight

I stared down the dusty road. There was still no one coming. We'd been walking alongside it for twenty minutes, and we hadn't seen a single vehicle.

My only hope was that the sloth had woken up and told the guard what he'd seen. That way the police could hold the villains at the East Station in Paris until we got there. It wasn't much of a hope.

Bones was examining the stony ground with his magnifying glass.

"I detect a slight rumble in those pebbles," he said. "Something's coming."

"At last!" said Otto. "Leave it to me."

A small blue car with a round roof spluttered around the bend, and Otto held out his paw to stop it.

It drew to a halt and a sheep stuck his head out of the window. He was wearing blue overalls and chewing a long blade of grass.

"I wonder if you could help me?" asked Otto. "We need to get to Paris urgently. Can you take us?"

The sheep stared at him with his mouth open, and the blade of grass fell down to his lap.

"I'm only going as far as the shearer's," he said.

"We really need your help," said Otto. "We're trying to foil the crime of the century!"

"Eh?" asked the sheep. He looked over to Bones and me in confusion. "What did you say?"

Otto sighed.

"I can see this is going to take a while," he said. "Indeed, you seem to be struggling. So, I'll tell you a secret — I have magic powers, and I'll use them against you if you don't let me borrow your car for the next two days. Let me demonstrate."

Otto took three separate metal rings out of his pocket and showed them to the sheep. He clanged the rings together, and they were instantly joined.

"Abracadabra!" he shouted.

"Hey," said the sheep. "How did you do that?"

"Magic," said Otto. "Now, I believe you have something in your ear."

He reached over to the sheep and pulled out a silver coin.

"Wait, what?" asked the sheep, patting the side of his head. "There were no coins in there."

In a rapid blur, Otto reached into his sleeve and swapped the real coin for a fake one. He then held up the fake coin and bit it in two.

The sheep looked at him with wide eyes and cowered back inside his car.

"I shall now disappear," said Otto. "And the same thing will happen to you if you disobey me."

He whipped out a smoke bomb and threw it to the ground. A cloud wafted up and he used it as cover to bolt around to the other side of the car.

As the smoke cleared, the sheep stuck his trembling head out of the window.

"Take my car!" he cried in an uneven voice. "Just don't let that cat vanish me!"

Complete the number chains to find the fastest route to Paris. The route with the smallest total is the quickest.

A.
7
× 4
+ 22
- 2
+ 11
= ?

B.
5
× 7
+ 9
÷ 2
+ 33
= ?

C.
9
× 3
+ 13
- 6
× 2
= ?

Otto jumped up and tapped on the passenger side window and the sheep yelped and leapt out, leaving his keys.

"Thank you," said Otto. "We promise to bring it back."

The sheep baaed and ran away down the road.

"Excellent work," I said, climbing into the front. "I'll drive."

Otto got into the passenger seat and picked up an old, yellowing road map.

"And I'll tell you the way," he said.

Bones got in the back, and we set off. I tried to speed up, but the car just chugged and spluttered along. It felt like the wheels would fall off if we went over a pothole.

"This is top speed?" I asked. "We couldn't even overtake those sloths."

"I'm afraid it's the only option we've got," said Otto. "Indeed, it is our only hope."

It was dark by the time we arrived in Paris. I decided to check the East Station first, just in case the guard had turned the criminals over to the police.

I parked in front of it and leapt out, leaving Bones and Otto in the car.

There was no sign of the criminals, or any police dogs, inside the station. There were only a few business animals on their way home.

I was about to head back when I spotted a couple of familiar faces. The sloths were sauntering across the station floor, dragging their cases behind them.

I rushed over to them.

"Hello," said the sloth who'd tried to rescue us. "Did you have a good journey?"

"No," I said. "Of course not. You saw us being attacked. Didn't you tell the guard?"

The sloth scratched his head.

"Oh yes," he said. "I remember that now. And there was me thinking I'd slept the whole way like usual."

"Well, I slept for the whole way," said the female sloth. "And I didn't even want to. I told the guard to wake me for breakfast, but she must've forgot."

If the sound of a bear pounding on the roof above her didn't wake her up, I doubted the guard would have had much chance.

"Did you see where the bear and moose went to?" I asked. "I need to stop them."

The sloth gestured vaguely ahead.

"They'll be somewhere in the city by now," he said, stifling a yawn. "We pulled in three hours ago."

"Three hours?" I cried. A shiver ran up my tail as I imagined what the villains were up to now. "What have you been doing since then?"

The sloth flopped his arm back over his shoulder.

"Getting here from platform 14," he said. "It's a long way, you know."

I left the sloths to their epic journey and ran back to the car.

Can you help the sloths get across the station?
They can only step on floor tiles that contain
multiples of 7 and are next to each other.

8	24	18	12	3
2	19	64	3	6
33	63	14	21	41
	28	1	56	35
	77	42	9	7
70	15	49	62	21
7	40	21	38	70
28	35	7	2	FINISH

"We're three hours too late," I said as I put my seatbelt back on.

"Head for the museum," said Bones. "The criminals may be meeting up with some accomplices before they steal the painting. We could still have time to stop them."

I put my foot down. The car shuddered and wheezed forward.

The Eiffel Tower, lit up by a thousand bulbs, appeared on our right.

"How wondrous is the City of Light," said Otto. "But what heavy hearts we bring to it. If only we were here to enjoy it rather than foil a villainous plot!"

"Speak for yourself," said Bones. "I love fighting crimes. Sightseeing, on the other hand, I can take or leave."

I screeched to a halt outside the Museum of Animal Arts, and we shot out. The building was made from thick limestone and had three long wings stretching around a wide courtyard with a fountain in the middle.

There were no lights on in the building, and no sign of anyone inside.

A police dog was strolling down the other side of the street, whistling to herself with her paws behind her back.

"You've got to help us!" I shouted. "It's about the *Mona Lemur.*"

She turned towards us, and tipped her hat up with the end of her truncheon.

"What about it?" she asked. "What's happened?"

"Nothing," said Bones. "Well, not yet. But it's going to be stolen tonight."

The dog gazed at us and scratched the side of her head.

"How do you know if it's not happened yet?" she asked.

"Because one of the criminals told me on stage," said Otto. "That is to say, I am a hypnotist and she was under my spell."

"I see," she said, chuckling to herself. "Well, thanks for letting me know."

She started to wander away again.

"We're telling the truth!" I cried. "You must believe us!"

"Okay," she said, still grinning. "I'll tell Hugo to keep an eye out. He's the police dog taking over when my shift ends."

She stuck her paws behind her back, and walked away, whistling again.

"She was no more use than the train guard," I said. "Why will no one take us seriously?"

Chapter Nine

We paced along the back wall of the museum, looking up at the windows. They were all closed.

"That could be worth a try," said Otto, pointing at a tiny gap at the bottom of a first-floor window.

"That?" I asked. "You could hardly get a breeze through there, let alone a cat."

Otto stretched his arms and feet out.

"That may be true for ordinary cats," said Otto. "But I have learnt the art of contortion. I've spent years squeezing myself into secret compartments. Lady and gentleman, watch this."

Otto crouched down, waggled his hips from side to side, and leapt into the air. I took a step back. I was convinced he was about to crash into the window and send glass showering down.

He landed on the ledge without a sound, pulled himself straight, and stuck his chin up until his head was a thin,

furry triangle. Then he shoved his paws into the tiny gap and dragged himself through as if he were a cat-shaped letter disappearing into a post box.

I know that cats can force themselves through surprisingly small gaps. My Aunt Ruby once beat a stingray in a limbo contest, for example. But even I'd never seen anything like this.

Otto grinned at us from behind the window, unhooked a latch, and pulled it up.

"Excellent work," said Bones.

Otto pulled a length of rope from his sleeve and dangled it down.

Bones climbed up and I followed. I could have jumped in without the rope, of course. But I was in no mood to show off my pouncing skills after Otto's display. I know when I can't compete.

"I haven't been in here since I solved the case of the six Napoleon squeaky toys," said Bones. "But I think I remember the way to the *Mona Lemur*. Follow me."

He led us through wide corridors flanked with paintings and sculptures. Most of the museum was completely dark, but there were spots where streetlamps shone in and gave us glimpses of the art.

Study the gallery scene on the previous page for two minutes, then see if you can answer the following questions.

1. How many paintings are there in the scene?

2. The cat on horseback was not wearing a hat – true or false?

3. Are there more cats or more dogs in the artworks altogether?

4. Which painting is the smallest?

5. There is a bunch of flowers in the pot – true or false?

I saw a huge oil painting of dogs in old-fashioned clothes jumping over a barricade and waving red, white and blue flags. In another, ancient Roman cats in togas were grasping swords and running into battle.

I was so distracted I almost bumped into a statue of a dog that was missing both of her arms. I gasped. This was the Venus de Fido, one of the most famous surviving sculptures from ancient Greece. I'd never have forgiven myself if I knocked her head off, too.

Bones led us into a gallery lined with paintings of animals wearing colourful doublets and breeches, and large, flat hats with feathers on.

"We must be getting close now," he said. "These Italian paintings date from the same time as the *Mona Lemur*."

He came to a halt facing a murky wall.

"Magnificent," he said.

I followed his gaze and saw the familiar orange eyes ringed with black, and the half-smile. We had reached the great painting itself.

"Isn't she beautiful?" asked Otto. "And isn't she a mystery? Is she happy? Is she sad? Is she feeling a bit funny after eating too many flowers?"

Staring at the artwork, I felt like I was being hypnotized all over again. First she seemed to be smiling, then frowning, then smiling again. It was a truly wondrous painting, and I could see why it meant so much to the animals of France.

I stood with my back to it, determined to do whatever I could to protect it.

Bones and Otto joined me and we stared silently into the gloom. I gazed at shadows until I imagined there was a bear and moose in each one. Then I'd blink, and realize we were still alone.

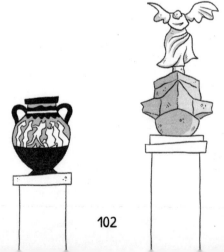

While you wait for the thieves to appear, can you work out which 11 pieces below fit together to make the Venus de Fido?

After an hour, I was sure I could hear something. A creaking sound, coming from our left. At first it was so faint I wondered if it were even in the museum at all. But it got louder, and I could hear panting, too.

"It's them," I whispered.

The pawsteps got closer. I crouched down and drew my claws. I held my breath, terrified that they'd hear me.

The dark shapes of the villains appeared in front of us.

"Now," whispered Bones.

I pounced on the figure at the front, while Bones and Otto took the one at the back.

The one I was tackling was wearing a hat, so I pulled it down over their eyes and pushed them over.

They yelped and struggled, but I managed to sit on them and hold their limbs down.

Even in the darkness, I knew something wasn't right. The animal I was squatting on was too small to be a bear or a moose. But I decided to stay put, at least until Bones and Otto had the other one under control.

It didn't sound like things were going too well for them, however. I heard Bones yelp and Otto cry, then someone run across the floor.

There was a click and everything went bright.

The criminal Otto and Bones were fighting had escaped and turned the light on.

Now I could see the figures, I realized they weren't actually criminals at all. They were police dogs.

I leapt off the back of mine and helped him to his feet.

"I am arresting you for attempting to steal the *Mona Lemur*," he said, wiping his neat blue uniform down.

"Stealing it?" I asked. "We were guarding it."

The other police dog strolled over with her paws behind her back.

"A likely story," she said. "Why would someone break into a museum to protect a painting?"

"Because we know who's going to take it," said Bones. "A bear and a moose. They're coming here tonight and we need to stop them."

The officer I'd fought took his hat off and beat the dust from it.

"We received a report that someone was about to steal the *Mona Lemur*," he said. "Bit of a coincidence that we found you here, isn't it?"

"No," I said. "Because we were the ones who told the other police dog about it. She was about to finish her shift, and she said she'd tell you about it. You're called Hugo, right?"

He exchanged a look of confusion with the other police dog.

"Yes," Hugo said. "But that proves nothing. Let's all go down to the station and get the Chief to sort this out."

"We need to stay here!" I cried. "This painting is going to be stolen!"

The police dog ignored me. He grabbed my wrist, and yanked me towards the exit.

Chapter Ten

Hugo marched us through the doors of the Paris central police station and into a large, bright room. Police dogs were sitting behind the desks that lined the walls. Some were scribbling in notebooks or clacking on typewriters, while others were examining plastic evidence bags that contained chewed tennis balls and sticks. There was a framed picture of a small basset hound on the wall behind them.

An elderly bloodhound with a gold badge on his jacket was sitting behind the largest desk. He waddled over to us, making his wobbly jowls smack together.

"We found these three trying to steal the *Mona Lemur,* Chief," said Hugo.

"We weren't trying to steal the painting," I said. "We were trying to protect it. A bear and a moose are going to take it tonight, and you need to let us go back there and stop them."

The Chief chuckled, sending ripples through his jowls.

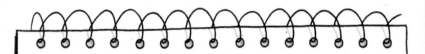

These police dogs are hard at work solving crimes. Can you spot the following pieces of evidence in the police station?

Tennis ball

Spotty collar

Squeaky bear

A pair of slippers

Broken vase

"I've met a lot of criminals in my time," he said. "But not a single one of them has told me about their crimes in advance. It would make my job a lot easier if they did."

The other police dogs looked up from their work and joined in with the giggling.

"That is because the circumstances are most unusual," said Otto. "Indeed, this may be one of the strangest cases you've ever encountered. Believe me when I say, ladies and gentlemen, that the bear revealed his plan to me while she was under hypnosis! For I am none other than the renowned magician, The Great Otto."

"And I'm Sherlock Bones," said Bones. "And I solve crimes. I don't commit them. I think you're going to need my help tonight, and I advise you let me go."

The Chief shook his head and pointed at me.

"We've already had The Great Otto and Sherlock Bones," he said. "Do you want to pretend to be the famous wolf detective Arsene Lupine before I throw you all in the cells?"

The other police dogs howled with laughter.

"You're making a mistake," cried Bones. "This nation's most beloved painting is about to be stolen! We want to help you!"

The Chief scratched his jowls.

"I'll tell you what," he said. "I'll send one of my officers down to the museum and get them to look out for bears, moose or snakes or whatever it was. If they catch anyone, I'll let you go free. In the meantime, let's find you all a nice, comfy cell."

The Chief walked us towards a door at the end of the room and down a corridor with grubby walls. There was a desk to our left, with a small door next to it.

A police bloodhound was slouching back with his feet on the desk. He whipped them down when he saw the Chief, and pretended to be doing some paperwork.

The Chief shoved us into the first of four empty cells. He pulled the iron door shut, locked it, and strolled away, chuckling to himself.

I clenched my paws. We were used to visiting criminals in prison, and it was awful to be on the wrong side of the bars. It felt so unfair when all we were doing was trying to protect a valuable painting.

"I suppose we'll just have to wait here and hope the police catch the bear and moose," I said.

"I don't think that's likely," said Bones. "None of the police have taken us seriously so far. As long as we're stuck in this cell, the painting isn't safe."

I sighed.

"There must be something we can do," I said.

"I'm afraid there's nothing you or I can do," said Bones. He looked over at Otto. "But I think our magician friend has a certain trick that could help."

Otto grinned and tapped the side of his nose.

"At your service," he said.

He pushed himself up to the bars and looked out at the guard.

"Excuse me?" he asked. "Could you help me with something?"

"What is it?" asked the guard, stepping over. "The Chief doesn't like me talking to prisoners."

Otto took out his pocket watch, shoved it between the bars, and swung it back and forth.

"Focus on the centre of the watch," he said. "You are feeling very sleepy. Your eyelids are heavy. You will close them when I click my fingers in five ... four ... three ... two ... one ..."

Otto clicked his fingers and the guard's shoulders drooped instantly. His pupils grew wide, and his mouth lifted into a faint smile.

"I wonder if we could have a look at your keys?" asked Otto.

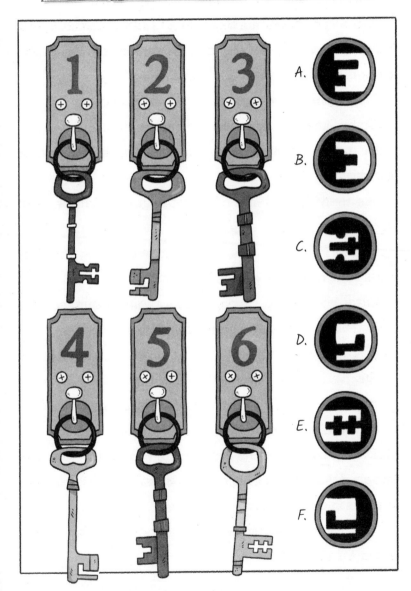

"Sure," said the guard. He threw them over, and Otto caught them.

"Go ahead and escape if you like," said the guard. "It will be worth it just to see the look on the Chief's face. I hate working for him."

Otto turned back to us.

"Some animals can't stop themselves telling the truth when they're under hypnosis," he said. "It's an interesting side-effect."

"He always shouts at me," said the guard. "I dipped my tail in his coffee once to get revenge, but he didn't notice."

"I'm sorry to hear this," said Otto, unlocking the iron door. "But right now we need your help, because the *Mona Lemur* is going to be stolen unless we can get out and save it. Is there a way we can leave this building without your chief spotting us?"

The guard pointed to the small door next to his desk.

"Yeah," he said. "That's the fire escape. It takes you down to a small alley. Follow it and take a right turn, and you'll be back on the main road. I never wanted to do this job, you know. I was the best pouncer in my class. I should have been in the dog Olympics, not stuck here."

"That is indeed a shame," said Otto.

He pushed the door open and we were free. I couldn't believe it. A few moments ago, I'd thought we'd be trapped in the cell all night, and now we were getting out. I wished we could bring Otto with us every time we were cracking a crime.

"One of your best shows yet," I said, as I stepped out. "Bravo."

The main door swung open and the Chief barged back in. He saw us and snarled, dripping drool onto the floor.

"What's going on in here?" he barked. "Get back in the cell!"

Chapter Eleven

The Chief turned to the guard and growled.

"How did you let this happen?" he asked. "Your one job is to make sure prisoners don't escape, and you haven't even managed that."

"Oh, shut up," said the guard. "I've had enough of you being mean to me. We all have. We call you 'Drooly' behind your back, you know."

"How dare you talk to your superior like that?" asked the Chief. "I should fire you on the spot."

"Go ahead if you want," said the guard. "I hate this job anyway."

The Chief turned to Otto.

"You've done something to my officer, haven't you?" he asked.

"I might have used my hypnotism skills on him," said Otto, spinning the keys on the end of his finger. "You should be pleased. Animals come from all over Europe to watch my performances, and you're getting one for free."

The Chief glared at us.

"Snap him out of it!" he cried. "Snap him out of it right now!"

"Fine," said Otto. He clicked his fingers.

The guard looked around and scratched his head. His pupils went back to normal size and his grin disappeared.

"Is everything alright, sir?" he asked. "I didn't see you come in."

"No, it is not," said the Chief. "I'll deal with you in a minute."

The Chief snatched the keys away from Otto.

"Right," he said. "You've shown that you can't be trusted. Now take out everything you're carrying and put it here."

He tapped his foot on the floor opposite our cell.

Otto reached into the inside pockets of his jacket and brought out his watch, a pack of cards, a rope, a wand, another pack of cards, a rose, a red sponge ball, a coin, a magnet, a false paw, two smoke bombs, three balloons, a third pack of cards, a pencil and a fake hammer. He tossed everything on to the floor, creating a huge pile.

"And the rest of it," said the Chief.

Otto sighed, reached into his sleeve, and pulled out a seemingly endless chain of knotted silk handkerchiefs.

"And the rest," said the Chief.

Otto lifted up his hat and pulled out a fake dove.

Otto takes four cards out of his pack and lays them facedown. He gives you four clues:

1. The value of a card on the left can't be greater than the value of the card to its right.

2. The difference between the first card and third card is 8.

3. The difference between the second card and fourth card is 7.

4. None of the cards have a value lower than 2 or higher than 10.

What are the numbers on the cards?

121

The Chief herded us back into the cell, locked the door and paced back to the guard.

"Excellent job, sir," said the guard.

"Don't bother crawling," said the Chief. "It's far too late for that. Now let's go and tell the others how stupid you were, so they don't make the same mistake."

The guard gulped and followed the Chief down the corridor. From the main room, I could hear the Chief shouting at the guard and telling the others to cover their ears if Otto tried to speak to them.

"Looks like you won't be using hypnosis on anyone else," I said, letting my shoulders droop. "Or any of your other tricks. But thanks for trying."

I clung on to the metal bars and stared at the wall opposite. Otto had come so close to setting us free, only to be interrupted by the Chief. If only we'd had a few seconds longer.

"Don't look so upset, Dr Catson," said Otto. "Things are never quite what they seem when there's a magician around."

Bones clapped his paws together and grinned.

"You mean you didn't hand over all your tricks?" he asked. "Let me guess. You have a secret compartment inside your hat containing dynamite to blast us free? Or you have a fake thumb that turns into a saw?"

"No," said Otto. "It's much simpler than that."

He lifted up his tongue and pulled out a key.

"Of course!" said Bones. "I should have guessed."

Otto turned the key in the lock and pushed the door open.

"You might have noticed that there were eight keys on the guard's chain," said Otto. "And yet there are four cells, meaning he keeps a spare of each one. I took the opportunity to slide one off earlier."

We ran out and Otto began to stuff his confiscated items back into his sleeve.

"We'd better go," I said. "You can pick up the rest of your things later."

Otto abandoned his props and followed us out of the fire exit.

"We'll have to take the backstreets in case the Chief sends some dogs out to look for us," said Bones. "This way."

Bones led us down winding alleys with cobblestones and street lamps. Every now and then the distant lights of the Eiffel Tower would appear in a narrow gap, then we'd take a sharp turn and they'd be gone again.

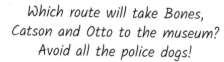

Which route will take Bones, Catson and Otto to the museum? Avoid all the police dogs!

124

We passed a café in which cats in berets were examining milk menus while stoat waiters scribbled in notepads, and a jazz club, where a Labrador in sunglasses was playing the piano and an audience of spaniels were howling along.

We crossed a busy road, cut through a courtyard, and arrived at the back of the museum.

"Look!" said Bones, pointing to a large open window ahead of us. "They're already inside!"

We leapt through the window and raced down the corridors into the long, gloomy gallery where we'd seen the *Mona Lemur.* I spotted the dark outline of a painting in the middle of the wall and let out a sigh of relief. We'd made it on time.

"Oh dear," said Otto, stepping closer. "This does not look right. Indeed, something has gone horribly wrong."

Bones flicked the light on.

What I saw made my heart race and my tail quiver. There was a portrait on the wall. But it wasn't the *Mona Lemur.* It was the terrible painting of the hairless cat from the train.

The criminals had stolen the most famous painting in the world. And they'd replaced it with the worst.

Chapter Twelve

"This is an insult to the entire nation of France," I said, looking at the horrible portrait that had taken the place of the *Mona Lemur*. "There'll be riots in the street if this gets out. It will make the French Revolution look like a pillow fight in kitten camp."

Bones examined the floor with his magnifying glass. He ran his fingers through a trail of white dust and looked up.

"The moose has scraped paint from the ceiling with his antlers," said Bones. "And it's fresh. They were here recently."

I raced ahead, following the thin trail along the wooden floor. It took me through a set of double doors and down a long corridor that spanned the north wing of the museum. Ancient plates and urns showing cats and dogs in tunics and togas whipped past me as I ran.

I swerved around a plinth with a marble horse on top, and I could see right to the end of the corridor.

There were three dark shapes approaching a door. The moose was there. I could just about make out his antlers in the gloom. The lumbering shape next to him must have been the bear. But there was someone else with them, someone very thin who was bobbing up and down.

I stepped on a creaky floorboard, and the thin figure turned to look at me.

"It's the polissssssse!" he hissed. "You ssssaid they wouldn't be here!"

The animals bolted through the door, and I could hear them thudding down stone steps.

I sprinted after them and reached the stairwell. They were already on the ground floor, scraping a fire door open. I pounced down the first set of stairs, crashed into the wall, then turned and leapt down the next one. By the time I got to the door, I felt like I'd been trampled by confused horses, but I'd caught up a little.

The bear was running through the wide park to the east of the museum, clutching

the painting to her chest, and the moose was just behind them, his antlers rustling the low branches of the trees.

The third animal was clearer now. It was a snake, slithering around the fountains and through the flower beds as it followed.

They seemed to be heading for a blue van, which was parked on the grass verge.

Bones and Otto hadn't even got out of the museum yet. If I was going to get the painting back, it would mean battling three criminals at once. I didn't stand much of a chance. But I had to do something. I couldn't let the *Mona Lemur* just slip away.

I threw myself into the air, flipping over a hedge, and balancing on the nose of a stone lion. Then I launched myself over a fountain, gliding so close that the water splashed my stomach.

Where have the criminals parked their van?
Follow the instructions below to find out
what to do at each landmark. Use the key
on the opposite page to help. The van you
end up at belongs to the thieves.

- At the gates, go south.

- When you reach the café, go east.

- When you reach the flower bed, go north.

- When you reach the statue, go east.

- At the oak tree, go south.

- At the fountain, go west.

- When you reach the boat lake, go south.

- At the sundial, go east until
  you reach the van.

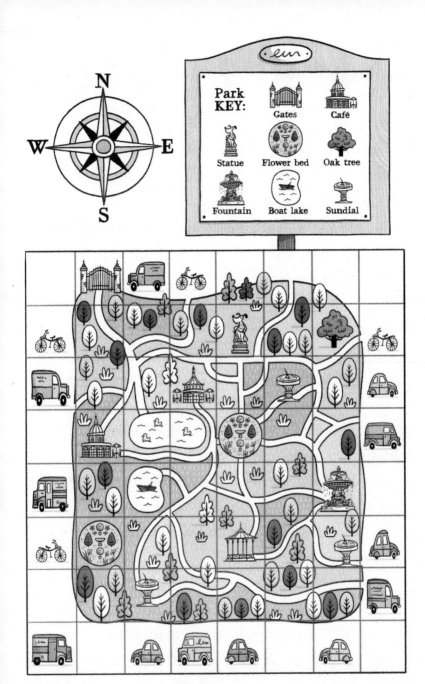

I landed on a patch of grass in time to see the bear open the back of the van and shove the painting inside. All three animals jumped into the front and they screeched away.

The van turned into a lane of traffic and I sprinted over to the pavement and followed it. If I could only get close to it, I might be able to open the back door and get the painting out before they noticed. But how could I catch up with a speeding van?

My heart hammered under my fur as I pushed myself harder and harder, but they disappeared into the distance.

The Eiffel Tower was ahead of me. Something about this view triggered a memory, but I couldn't place it. It wasn't easy to think straight when I was trying to outrun traffic.

Then I realized. I'd seen this exact street when Otto had hypnotized me. I'd been chasing an actual lemur, rather than a van containing the *Mona Lemur*, but otherwise it was the same.

In my vision, I'd taken a shortcut to my right, and caught up with the lemur at a crossroads. Is this what I had to do now? If Bones had been here, he'd have told me to stop being such a silly kitty. There's no way my hypnotized brain could have given me clues about the future.

But Bones wasn't here, and I only had my instinct to rely on.

I swung into a side street with high stone buildings on each side. An alleyway appeared on my left, then another to my right. I zigzagged through them, letting the memory of my vision guide me.

I emerged at a crossroads. It looked just like the one I'd seen while I was hypnotized, with the green newspaper kiosk on the corner.

A van was approaching, and I saw the dark outline of antlers in the passenger seat. My instinct had been right.

The van stopped at a red light and I crept over to the doors at the back. I turned the handle, and pulled it open. I could see the frame of the *Mona Lemur* inside, dumped on top of the suitcase Otto had been imprisoned in.

I was about to grab it when the lights changed, and the bear stepped on the gas. The van drove off, leaving me clinging to the handle as the door banged wide open.

"Intruder!" shouted the moose.

"Sssssshake them off!" hissed the snake.

The van swerved from side to side, making the other drivers bark and honk their horns. A giraffe who was driving next to us opened his sunroof and stuck his head out.

"Fool!" he cried.

"Sorry," I shouted, clinging to the handle with both paws. "But I'm on very important business."

The van cut in front of the giraffe's car, and turned right into another street. I was swung out so violently that my tail smacked into a road sign.

I reached out with my right paw. If I could only get hold of the edge of the door, I could propel myself into the van and get the painting.

The bear skidded the van to the left, and the door slammed shut with a loud snap. I winced, imagining how it would have felt if my paw had been in there.

I was scrabbling around with the handle and trying to get the door open again, when I heard a loud bang and found myself flat against the metal. I felt as though someone had smacked me in the face with the world's biggest frying pan. A second later, I was on the road, and the sounds of screeching brakes and honking horns were all around me.

I was dazed for a few moments, and tried to piece together what had happened. The van was still ahead of me, but it had stopped moving. I felt my face and body. Nothing was broken, though everything was sore.

"Get out of my way!" the bear was yelling. "I'm too busy for this!"

I got to my feet and hobbled around to the front of the van. In her frantic attempts to shake me off, the bear had crashed into a black car.

A Rottweiler in a smart suit had stepped out of it and was barking at her.

The bear reached into her pocket, pulled out a wad of banknotes and held them out to the dog.

"Take this for the damage," she said. "And move along!"

"And let you ruin someone else's car?" asked the Rottweiler. "Not likely! You deserve to be in prison for the way you were driving!"

Cars had pulled up all around us, trapping the criminals. A pangolin, a beaver and a gopher stepped out to watch. Soon, dozens of animals had gathered around the smashed car and van.

"This bear needs to be locked up!" shouted the dog.

I noticed a thin shape on the road. The snake had slithered out, and was approaching the Rottweiler with his head back and his fangs out.

"Watch out!" I cried, pointing at the snake.

The Rottweiler yelped and jumped back. He grabbed the snake around the tail and head.

"Did you see that?" he asked, lifting the snake up to the crowd. "He tried to bite me!"

Gopher   Pangolin   Cat   Beaver   Rottweiler

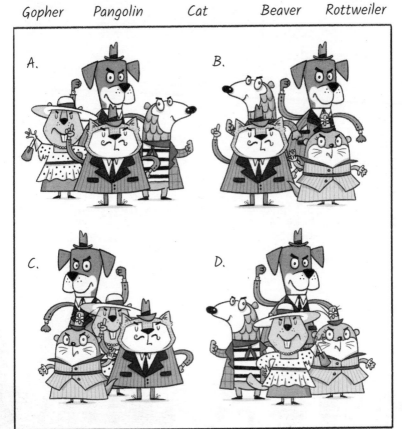

A.

B.

C.

D.

I heard a siren behind us, and blue light flooded the scene. A police van pulled up behind the criminals, blocking them in. The passenger door opened and I expected to see another police dog emerge. But what I saw made me gasp. Bones stepped out, followed by Otto.

"Excellent work, Catson," said Bones.

A police bloodhound got out of the driver's seat and opened the back door. A small basset hound with bushy, white eyebrows stepped out. He was wearing a police cap, and a jacket covered in medals and ribbons.

"Well, then," he said to Bones. "Let's have a look at it."

Bones opened the doors at the back of the van, lifted the *Mona Lemur* out, and handed it to the basset hound.

"Good heavens," said the dog, taking a pair of glasses out of his jacket pocket and examining the painting. "It's the real thing."

The bear and moose stepped out of their van.

"Thank goodness you're here," said the moose. He pointed at me. "We caught this cat trying to steal the *Mona Lemur*. Luckily, we got it back from her, and we were returning it to the museum."

I felt my muscles tightening and my tail twitching. How could the criminals still be keeping up their ridiculous lies after they'd been caught red-pawed?

"That's complete nonsense!" I cried. "They were heading away from the museum, not towards it!"

The Rottweiler ran over, still holding the snake.

"That bear just smashed my car," said the Rottweiler. "Then she tried to bribe me, and this snake tried to attack me."

"Liesssss," hissed the snake.

The onlookers crowded around the officer, giving their version of events.

The basset hound took a whistle out of his pocket and blew it.

"That's enough yapping from everyone," he said. "I need to think. First, I'm told this bear, moose and snake stole the *Mona Lemur*. Now I'm being told this cat took it. Who on earth is telling the truth?"

The bear stuck her paw up.

"We can sort it out at the local police station if you like," she said. "We'd hardly want to go there if we were guilty, would we?"

"Very well," said the basset hound. "Everyone get in my van!"

The police bloodhound led us round to the back door of the van and opened it for us. I sat on the left with Bones and Otto, while the snake, the bear and moose sat opposite and scowled at us. Their weight made the van tip slightly.

The police dog got into the front, and the basset hound, still clutching the *Mona Lemur*, sat in the passenger seat.

"Oh dear," I said, as we drove off. "Now we're being taken back to the very place we just escaped from. This can't be good."

Bones tapped the side of his nose.

"Don't worry, my dear Catson," he said. "We're going exactly where we need to be."

Chapter Thirteen

The police bloodhound marched us into the entrance hall of the police station.

The Chief was sitting behind his desk at the far wall. He leapt up and ran towards us, his saggy mouth lifting into a smile.

"Excellent," he said. "I see you've found our criminals."

The bear, moose and snake walked in, and his smile drooped. The basset hound walked in next, with the *Mona Lemur* in his paws, and the Chief's jowls began to tremble.

"Good evening, Commissioner," he said, bowing. "And ... er ... what are you doing here?"

144

A.

B.

C.

D.

"I'm hoping to find out how this priceless painting ended up in the back of a van," said the basset hound.

The Chief jabbed his finger towards us.

"Those thieves took it," he said. "We caught them trying to grab it earlier, and put them in the cells. But they escaped and went back for another try. Now you've caught them, we can lock them up for good."

"See?" said the bear. "We were telling the truth. Now if you just hand the painting over, we'll put it back in the gallery, as we were trying to do all along."

The bear made a grab for the painting, but the Commissioner stepped back.

"Hand that over and you'll never see it again," said Bones. "These thieves will sell it to a private collector and it will be lost to your country forever."

"You've no right to call Harold, Benjamin and Marie thieves!" yelled the Chief. "They're respectable animals, unlike you."

Bones gazed at the Chief and rubbed his chin.

"Out of interest, how do you know the names of these animals?" asked Bones. "Have you met them before?"

The Chief squirmed and looked down at his feet.

"Probably," he said. "I can't remember."

The bear and moose grimaced and inched back towards the door. But two of the police bloodhounds stepped behind and blocked them.

"Perhaps you'd like me to refresh your memory," said Bones. "You know these animals because you're secretly working with them. A few days ago, you sent them a letter agreeing to let them steal the *Mona Lemur* in exchange for a bribe."

The other police dogs gasped and stared at the Chief with wide eyes.

The Chief growled at Bones, sending ripples through his jowls.

"How dare you accuse me of such a serious crime in front of my commissioner?" he barked. "You're going to be locked up for a very long time for that."

The Chief turned to the dogs behind him.

"Get these criminals cuffed and back in the cell," he said.

The dogs stood up, but the Commissioner held his paw up to stop them.

"Not just yet," he said. "I want to hear what they've got to say for themselves."

Bones placed his paws behind his back and paced around the space between the desks.

"We were brought here earlier this evening and accused of stealing the *Mona Lemur*," said Bones. "We had, in fact, been protecting it. I told the Chief that a bear and moose were planning to steal it, and he replied that he knew nothing about any bears, moose and snakes. This instantly made me

suspicious, as I hadn't mentioned a snake, and didn't yet know that one was involved."

"That proves nothing!" yelled the Chief. "Everyone knows burglars send snakes in through drainpipes to open doors and windows for them. Of course they'd have been using a snake. If they'd done it. Which they didn't."

The snake reared his head back and hissed, dripping venom on the floor.

"I thought back to when I'd first heard about the crime," said Bones. "The bear had mentioned getting a letter from 'the boss'. I assumed this meant the head of their criminal gang, but I now wondered if it had actually referred to the local police chief."

The Chief was growling, and his floppy ears were shaking. He looked as though he was about to lunge forward and bite Bones.

"We escaped the cell and returned to the museum," said Bones. "We found the painting gone, and the criminals fleeing the scene. Catson raced ahead to catch them, leaving Otto and me behind. I glanced out of the window and saw them getting into a van with a snake, and I knew I was right. The Chief knew more about the criminals than we did, because he was in league with them."

Otto skipped across the floor, waving his paws around wildly.

"Bones explained his suspicions to me, and we were at a loss," said Otto. "That is to say, we were stumped. We couldn't catch up with the criminals, and we couldn't return to the police station. It was at this point that I suggested we visit the police headquarters and speak to the most honoured and respected police dog in all the country.
That is to say, you, sir, of course."

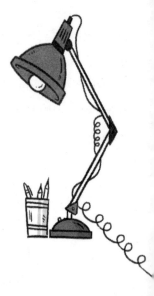

Otto came to a stop behind the Chief's desk. He looked at the Commissioner and bowed down low, rolling his right paw ahead of him.

The Chief fixed his eyes on the Commissioner and pointed at Otto.

"And how did this trickster persuade you to leave your important work in such a hurry?" he asked.

The Commissioner stared into the distance for a moment.

"I was at my desk," he said. "These animals came in, and the cat asked me to look at his watch. Then we were driving around and looking for a blue van with the *Mona Lemur* inside."

"He hypnotized you," said the Chief. "He did the same thing to my guard earlier this evening, which is how they all managed to escape."

Otto strode forwards.

"I'm afraid that part is true," he said. "I wouldn't usually use my stage skills in real life, but this was an emergency. That is to say, I had no choice."

"See?" asked the Chief. "He's brainwashed you. He has no evidence for anything he's saying. None of them do."

Otto took his hat off and pulled out a thick brown envelope.

"As a matter of fact, I think I might," he said. "A few seconds ago, I managed to swipe this from your desk drawer. It has 'For the Chief' written on it. Shall we see what's inside?"

Otto opened the envelope and three wads of banknotes tumbled down to the floor.

The Commissioner stared at it with his mouth open. Several of the watching police dogs let out barks of shock.

"He's planted that evidence," growled the Chief. He was sweating and panting as if he'd just fetched a very large stick. "It's yet another of his magic tricks. Don't fall for it."

The snake shrieked and made a leap for a high window to the right of the door, but a police bloodhound grabbed him and yanked him back down.

Bones wandered over to the Chief's desk and pulled the drawer open. He took out a piece of paper and examined it with his magnifying glass.

"To-do list," he read. "'1. Send letter to Marie telling her to go ahead. 2. Collect envelope full of money. 3. Spend money on deluxe dog basket'."

"A coincidence," said the Chief. "He's twisting my words."

Bones rifled around and pulled out a small book.

"And this appears to be a secret diary," he said. "It reads, 'Received bribe today. I love bribes. Must line up some more bribes soon.'"

"You fool," muttered the bear, staring at the Chief and shaking her head.

The moose made a run for the door, but two of the police dogs grabbed him and twisted his arms behind his back.

"I've heard enough!" shouted the Commissioner. He turned to the Chief. "I am arresting you for accepting bribes."

He dashed over to a group of police dogs near to the door and handed the *Mona Lemur* to them.

"Get this back in the museum right away," he said.

He turned to face the others.

"The rest of you stay here and help me put the criminals in their cells," he said. "Starting with your boss."

The Chief threw his head back and let out a long howl.

Chapter Fourteen

We helped Otto gather the rest of his things from the floor, while the police dogs showed the criminals to their cells.

"Well done for finding the bribe," said Bones. "I thought you were up to something with that elaborate bow."

"A simple distraction technique," said Otto. "Make an extravagant movement with the right paw so nobody looks at the other one."

He bent low and waved his right paw again. When he stood up, a red rose had appeared in his left one.

"Amazing," I said. "I wish you could show me how to do all that stuff. It would be so useful when cracking crimes."

Otto paused in the middle of stuffing the chain of handkerchiefs up his sleeve.

"I'm afraid it goes against the code of the magician to use our skills offstage," said Otto. "I only did so because it was a dire emergency, and I would never teach tricks to anyone who planned to use them in everyday life."

The Chief was grabbing the bars of his cell and growling, while the bear and moose were lying on their beds and staring at the ceiling.

The guard shoved the snake into the final cell and locked the door. The snake slid out between two of the bars and hissed at him.

"Letting animals escape again?" asked the Chief. "You don't learn, do you?"

"Excuse me?" asked the guard. "You're my prisoner now. You'd better watch what you say if you want your evening dog biscuits."

The Chief looked down and whimpered.

The guard grabbed the snake and shoved him into a bucket. He placed it upside down in the cell, trapping him inside.

"There," he said. "Wriggle out of that."

"Let me out," hissed the snake. "I'm innosssent. I only opened the door for them. I didn't know they were going to ssssteal anything."

It normally takes the Chief nine seconds to eat one dog biscuit. How long would it take him to eat all the biscuits in this jar?

The Commissioner strode in, followed by a police bloodhound carrying the terrible portrait of the hairless cat.

"The *Mona Lemur* is safely back where she belongs," he said. He pointed at the picture. "My dogs found this in the museum. Know where it came from?"

"As a matter of fact, I do," said Bones. "It belongs to this bear and moose."

He carried a chair to the wall opposite their cells, and propped the painting on it.

"I'm going to leave it right here for them to enjoy," he said. "They paid a lot of money for it, so it's only fair they should get to look at it."

The bear and moose scowled at us as we walked away.

We spent the next morning exploring Paris with Otto. At noon, we climbed a hill, bought some spider croissants, and ate them while looking down at the city. The straight, wide streets and winding alleys were laid out before us, with the museum to our right and the Eiffel Tower rising in the distance.

"All is well with this great city once more," said Bones. He turned to Otto. "And it's all thanks to your wonderful illusion skills."

"I never could have done it without your help," said Otto. "Indeed, I would still be trapped inside that suitcase."

Otto finished the last of his croissant, turned to face us, and bowed.

"And now, lady and gentleman, it's time for me to vanish for real," he said. "I promised I'd return the sheep's car, and I intend to do so. That is to say, I always keep my word."

He whipped a smoke bomb out of his sleeve and threw it to the ground. When the wind blew the smoke away, he was nowhere to be seen.

"These stage performers always have to be so dramatic," I said. "It's a shame we couldn't shake his paw and say a proper goodbye."

"I think it's time for us to say goodbye to the city, too," said Bones. "We should have just enough time to make it to the North Station and get the next train to Calais."

We got up and walked through a square lined with busy cafés. Stoat waiters were scurrying around and serving fresh bread flavoured with spices and insects to hedgehogs, foxes and rabbits.

The middle of the square was filled with artists selling paintings of local landmarks. Some had set up easels and were offering to sketch passing animals in charcoal.

Most of the artworks were brilliant, but I spotted a stall selling absolutely terrible ones. It was no surprise to see the artists were the same ones we'd met on the train. The hairless cat and the polecat were offering wonky landscapes that looked like they'd been painted by blindfolded moles, while the wombat was sketching a German shepherd who was sitting for him.

I felt my fur prickle as I remembered how unhelpful these artists had been.

"Let's go and tell that lot what we think of them," I said. "Those criminals almost got away with it thanks to them."

"Leave them be," said Bones. "It looks like their lack of talent will be its own punishment."

A group of beagles were pointing and laughing at their paintings, and the hairless cat was scowling and flushing red. The wombat finished his sketch of the German shepherd, who looked at it, growled, and hit him over the head with it.

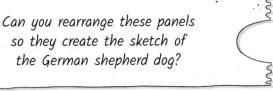

Can you rearrange these panels so they create the sketch of the German shepherd dog?

A.   B.   C.   D.   E.   F.   G.   H.

"I don't think Paris appreciates their genius after all," said Bones. "I only hope they've kept enough money for their train tickets back."

We continued across the square, and made our way down the hill. I thought back over all the strange things that had happened to us since Otto's magic show.

"Well done for bringing the Chief and the other criminals to justice," I said. "But this is one case in which you weren't right about everything."

Bones stopped and fixed his eyes on me.

"What on earth do you mean?" he asked.

"I saw the streets of Paris when I was hypnotized," I said. "And you said it didn't mean anything. But it was actually a helpful vision, and it showed me the shortcut I needed to take in real life."

Bones snorted out a laugh.

"Don't be ridiculous," he said. "Whatever you think you saw, I'm sure it was nothing more than a coincidence."

I knew there was no point arguing with Bones, but I also knew what I'd seen. Maybe there was a little more real magic in the world than he was prepared to admit.

We got to the station with five minutes to spare, and I was pleased to see the train was so empty we could have a whole compartment to ourselves. There would be much less chance of drama this time.

Soon, the doors were closed, and the guard blew his whistle. I was waiting for the steam to chug out, but I heard shouting from the platform instead.

I looked out of the window and saw the sloths were struggling towards us, dragging their cases with their teeth gritted. I got up, swung the door open and pulled them up to the train.

The whistle blew again, and this time we were off.

The sloths ambled into our compartment and I lifted their cases up to the rack.

"Thank you," said the male sloth, as they climbed on to the seats.

"No problem," I said. "Did you have a nice time in Paris?"

"Not really," he said. "We've spent the whole time since we last saw you rushing here from the other station. We should have left more than a day for the connection. What about you?"

I looked out of the window and got a last glimpse of the Eiffel Tower as we chugged away.

"It's a long story," I said. "It all started when I agreed to be hypnotized by The Great Otto as part of his magic show in Berlin. I didn't think it would work on me, but something very strange happened ..."

I looked back at the sloths and saw they both had their eyes closed, and were snoring peacefully.

Bones had tipped his hat down over his eyes and was napping, too. I was feeling pretty exhausted myself, now I came to think of it. I closed my eyes and rested my head back on the seat. I drifted into a deep sleep, hoping I'd have no more visions of dark city streets ... or lemurs.

ANSWERS

THANKS FOR HELPING
US CRACK THE CASE.

Chapter One

Page 9
11 handkerchiefs
8 doves
13 playing cards

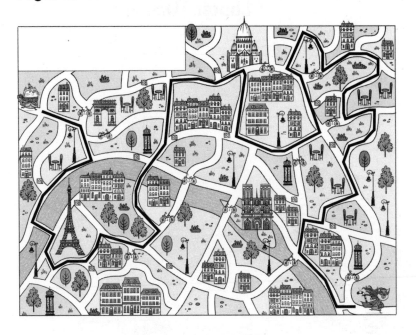

Chapter Two

Page 21

Page 25
Tiles B, C, D, E and G match the view exactly.
Tiles A, F and H do not.

Chapter Three

Page 32

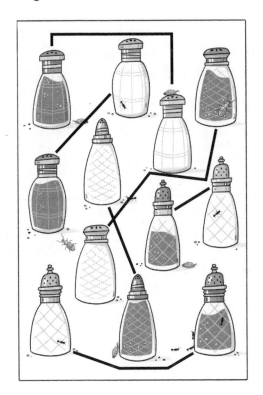

Page 36

The letters can be rearranged to spell STATUE.
The attraction the bear is looking at is the Venus de Fido.

Chapter Four

Pages 46-47

The weasel painted the landscape (A)
The hairless cat painted the fruit bowl (C)
The wombat painted the portrait of the hairless cat (B)
The polecat painted the seaside (D)

Page 49

To cut the loaf into 8 equal pieces using 3 cuts, the lynx must:

1. Cut the loaf in half
2. Make a second cut to cut the loaf into quarters
3. Finally, cut the loaf sideways through the middle to create 8 even pieces.

Chapter Five

Pages 54–55
Crunchy ant croissant = €6
Herb omelette = €8
Grass-flavoured yoghurt = €7
Slice of melon = €3

Page 62
Silhouette D matches the moose exactly.

Chapter Six

Page 67

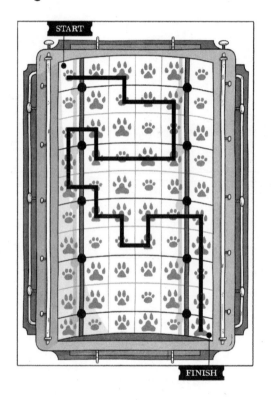

Page 70

The train went through tunnel C.

Chapter Seven

Page 75

Page 78

A = 7,G
B = 6,E
C = 4,C
D = 3,F
E = 6,B

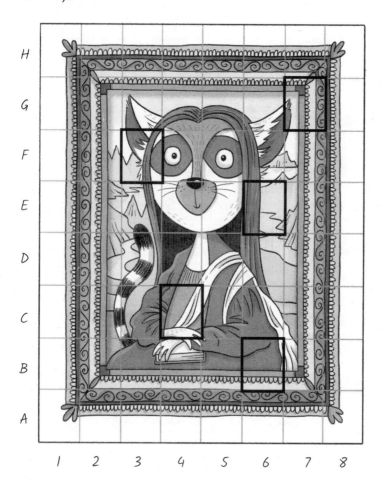

Chapter Eight

Page 86

A. 7 × 4 + 22 - 2 + 11 = 59
B. 5 × 7 + 9 ÷ 2 + 33 = 55
C. 9 × 3 + 13 - 6 × 2 = 68

Pages 90–91

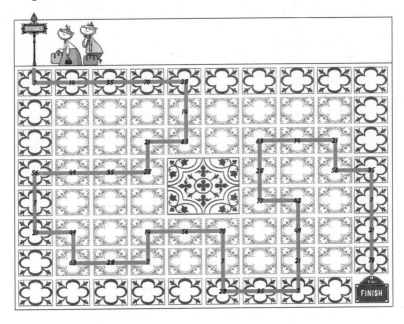

Chapter Nine

Pages 99–100

1. There are 4 paintings in the scene.

2. False - the cat on horseback was wearing a hat.

3. There are more cats than dogs in the paintings altogether. There are 5 cats in the artworks and 3 dogs.

4. The top-right painting is the smallest painting.

5. False - there are no flowers in the pot.

Chapter Ten

Pages 110–111

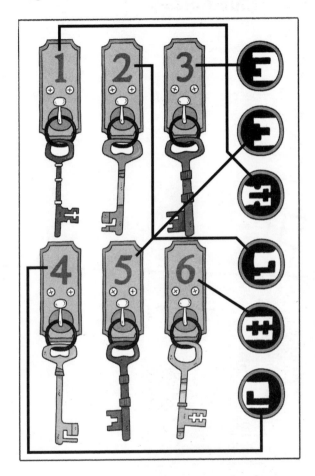

Chapter Eleven

Page 121

The first card is 2. The second card is 3. The third card is 10. The fourth card is also 10.

Page 124

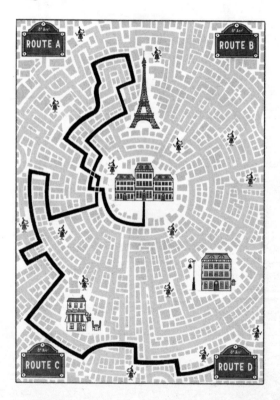

Chapter Twelve

Pages 130-131

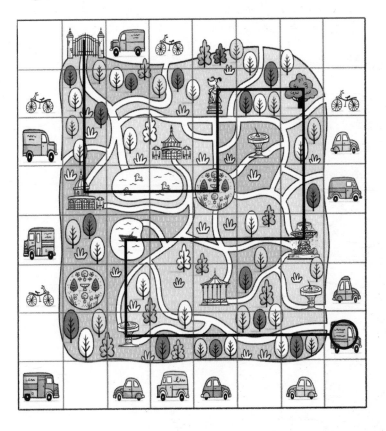

Page 137

A = Gopher is missing

B = Beaver is missing

C = Pangolin is missing

D = Cat is missing

Chapter Thirteen

Pages 144–145
Set D matches the medals on the Commissioner's jacket exactly.

Page 153
There are 20 banknotes in the jumble on the floor.

Chapter Fourteen

Page 159

There are 15 biscuits in the jar.

15 x 9 = 135.

It would take the Chief 135 seconds, or 2 minutes 15 seconds, to eat all the biscuits in the jar.

Page 163

The panels need to be rearranged in the following order: C, F, B, H, D, A, E, G

The sketch would look like this:

The End!

Also available:

Help Bones and Catson solve another mystery in

Sherlock Bones and the Case of the Crown Jewels

When the crown jewels go missing from Kennel Palace, it's up to super-sleuth Sherlock Bones and his trusty sidekick Dr Jane Catson to solve the crime. But with multiple suspects and a trail that's starting to run cold, will they be able to catch the culprit in time?

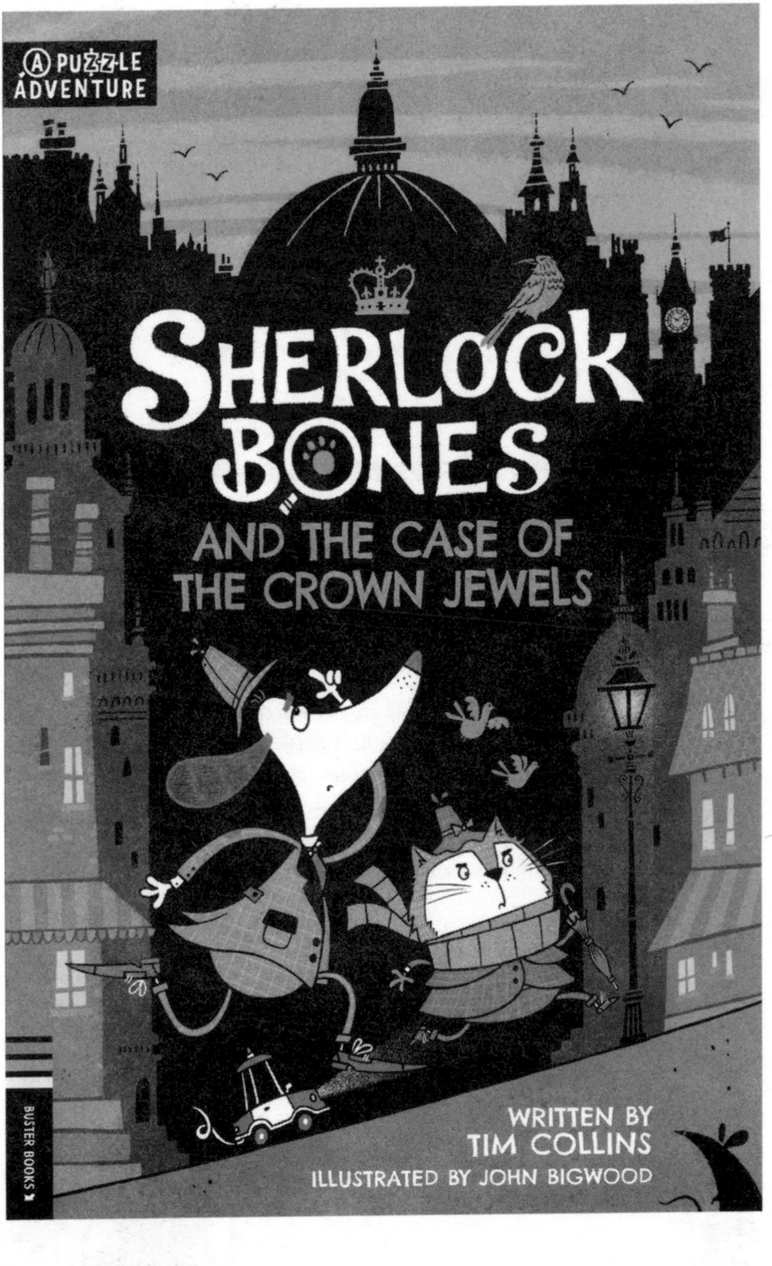

A PUZZLE ADVENTURE

SHERLOCK BONES

AND THE CASE OF THE CROWN JEWELS

WRITTEN BY
TIM COLLINS
ILLUSTRATED BY JOHN BIGWOOD

BUSTER BOOKS

Also available:

**Help Bones and Catson
solve another mystery in**

*Sherlock Bones and the
Curse of the Pharaoh's Mask*

Sherlock Bones and Dr Jane Catson are taking
a well-earned holiday in Egypt when they
discover that a precious mask has been stolen
— and they are the suspects! Can Bones and
Catson escape the tombs of the ancient cat
kings and catch the true thief in time?

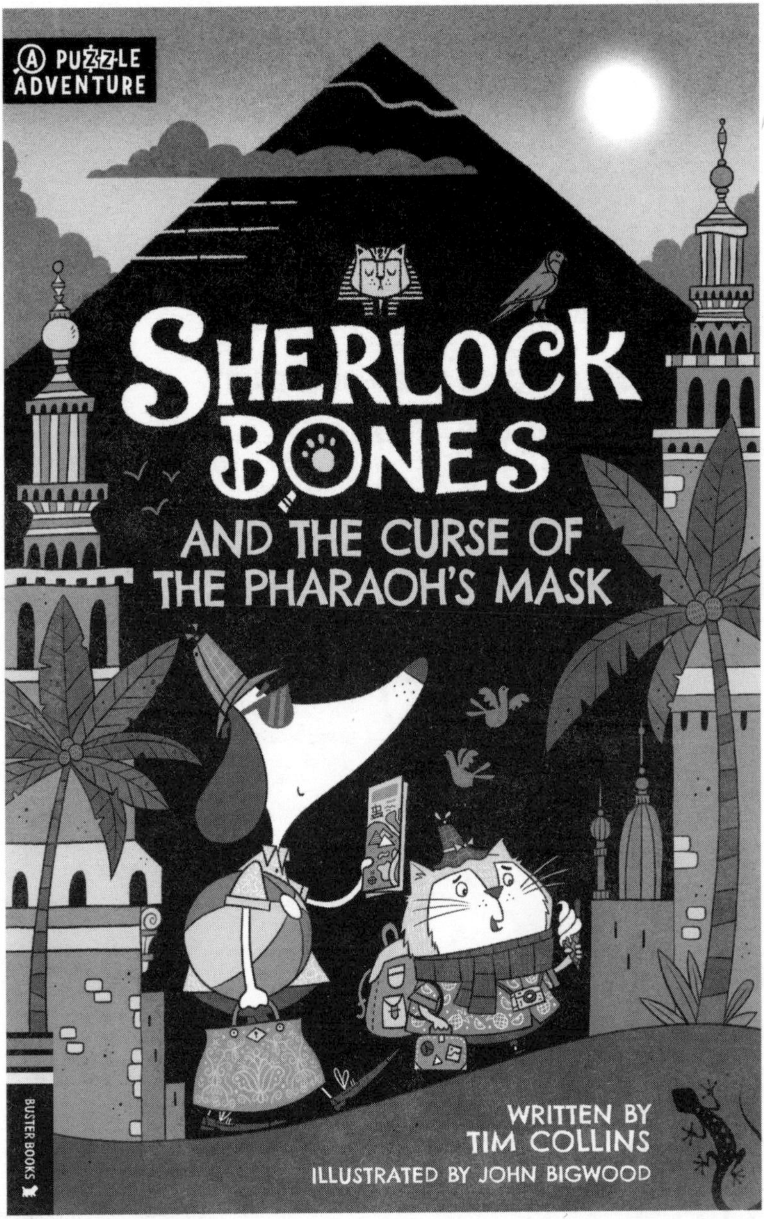

A PUZZLE ADVENTURE

SHERLOCK BONES

AND THE CURSE OF THE PHARAOH'S MASK

WRITTEN BY
TIM COLLINS

ILLUSTRATED BY JOHN BIGWOOD

BUSTER BOOKS

Publishing in Autumn 2023:

*Sherlock Bones and the
Horror of the Haunted Castle*